pool boy

pool boy

michael simmons

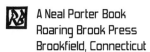
A Neal Porter Book
Roaring Brook Press
Brookfield, Connecticut

A Neal Porter Book
Published by Roaring Brook Press
A division of The Millbrook Press, 2 Old New Milford Road,
Brookfield, Connecticut 06804

Library of Congress Cataloging-in-Publication Data
Simmons, Michael
Pool boy / Michael Simmons. — 1st ed.
p. cm.
"A Neal Porter Book."
Summary: When his father is arrested for insider trading and his family
loses all their money, Brett Gerson takes a job as an assistant to a
70-something pool cleaner in his former wealthy California neighborhood
and learns some valuable life lessons.
[1. Fathers and sons—Fiction. 2. Wealth—Fiction. 3. Prisoners—Fiction.
4. Family life—California—Fiction. 5. California—Fiction.] I. Title.
PZ7.D5158 Po 2003
[Fic] —dc21   2002012983

ISBN 0-7613-1885-2 (trade edition)
10 9 8 7 6 5 4 3 2

ISBN 0-7613-2924-2 (library binding)
10 9 8 7 6 5 4 3 2 1

Book design by Jaye Zimet
Printed in the United States of America

First edition

For my family

Acknowledgments

The author wishes to thank Anne Dahlie, Elizabeth Dahlie, Patrick Daley, Kim Feltes, Eloise Flood, Christopher Miller, George Nicholson, Neal Porter, and Paul Rodeen.

pool boy

1 It's like this. I used to be one of those kids who could coast through life without having to do any of the unpleasant things most people have to do. I'm fairly smart, pretty athletic, and some have even told me I'm reasonably handsome. The key to the cushy life I used to lead was that I also used to be rich. Not fairly, or pretty, or reasonably, but extremely. Extremely rich. All

that changed one day when cops and guys in suits showed up at my house and told my dad that he was in big trouble and that he owed the U.S. government ten million dollars.

Dad tried to run. He pushed one of the cops and tried to make a getaway out the back. It's actually funny when you think about it. Eight armed cops and my dad tries to outrun them through the kitchen. He got as far as the stove before a bald guy they called Pointy tackled him to the ground. I guess it wasn't funny at the time, what with my mom and my sister crying hysterically and my dad's face bleeding. But it's sure funny now, now that it's over and now that I hate him.

My mother says that Dad's a different kind of criminal. He's a white-collar criminal, which she says means he didn't really hurt anyone. (Anyone but me, I always say.) But they still threw him in jail. Our rip-off artist of a lawyer said he'd be in less trouble if he hadn't tried to run.

The thing is that Dad never really acted like a criminal. He laughed a lot, always kept his hair neatly combed, always wore a suit and tie, blah blah blah. And he had a smile that made you trust him, made you think everything would be all right. He even cried when they finally carted him off. That's something you never see in the movies—a bad guy who cries when the cops nab him. That was a rough thing to see. That was probably the hardest thing of all—watching Dad cry as cops threw him into the back of a squad car. Don't get me wrong. Right now, I hate the guy. But that was rough.

But enough about him. He blew it and now he has to live with it. So let me tell you what's really unfair: the fact that I, an entirely innocent human being, had to give up my easy life. I know, plenty of people live happy lives without being loaded. But if you go from the life of leisure that I once had, to the life of toil and drudgery that I have now, it's very, very hard.

My mom even forced me to get a job. She said I needed to start a college fund. Let me tell you what I really need: my old life back. That's it. I don't need college and I don't need a job. I need a house with a pool, and an expensive stereo, and a beach house. Just so I'm clear, let me say that I now have none of these things.

2 It's not like I thought I'd never have to work. But I planned to put it off until after I went to business school. And I even imagined that I might have to scrimp and save a bit. My best friend Frank and I were planning a trip to Mexico for the summer after we graduated from high school. We were

going to live by our wits, sleep on the beach, surf all day, and catch fish for dinner. Maybe we'd live like that forever. Never come home. Now life on the cheap doesn't seem so exciting.

When my dad was first carted off, my family tried to be hush-hush about it. "We have to keep up appearances," my mother kept saying. My sister and I continued going to school, playing sports, attending class dances like nothing had happened. My mother even decided to go ahead with an addition we were building on our house. "We don't want people to think anything's wrong," she said. But when a huge article about my father was finally plastered on the front page of the *Glenwood Times,* people didn't have to spend time wondering what was up with the Gerson family. It was all there in black and white.

After our contractor read the story, he told my mom he was going to bill her for the work he had already done on the addition. He said he billed all his customers this way—bit by bit. My mom was pretty mad after he left. "He's never billed anyone like that in his life," she yelled. "He just wants to make sure he gets his money."

Guess what. She was right. He did want to get his money. And he was right to be worried, cause we haven't paid him a dime. We still owe him. Now the beautiful, happy suburb of Glenwood, California, knows that the Gersons are a bunch of welchers.

"Can't you ask your grandparents for money?" my best friend Frank asked one afternoon by his pool after I finally told him what was going on.

"My grandparents?" I said. "Two are dead and the other two live in Maine and haven't got a nickel. The only one in my family who ever got rich was my dad."

Getting rich was, in fact, something Dad took lots of pride in. He loved to talk about how he was a big-time stockbroker and made lots of money. "Gerson boy makes good," he used to say every time he bought something big. He said it the time he bought a boat, the time he drove home a new Mercedes, and the day he bought our beach house.

He doesn't say it now.

"You must have some money somewhere," Frank said, after thinking it over for a few minutes.

I wanted to hit him. But I forgave him for this stupid remark because it's exactly what I said over and over to my mother.

"We must have some money somewhere," I kept saying. But she only shook her head.

"I know this is hard for you to understand," she told me. "It's hard for me to understand. But even after we sell everything we have, we're still in debt. We've got nothing." She said this and then started crying for the hundred-and-fiftieth time. Funny, after watching your mother cry one hundred and fifty times, it doesn't get any easier. It always hurts. And I'm sure it'll hurt after I see it for the thousandth time.

3 So let me tell you what my family does have besides a jail-bird dad and a mound of debts. We have a crazy aunt. When you're coasting by on your looks and your dad's cash, a crazy aunt doesn't seem very useful. But crazy aunts almost always have big houses where poor relatives can go to live. My aunt has no money, and no swimming pool. She doesn't even own a car. But my aunt has a big house. Or she has a house that was big enough for my mother, my sister, and me to live in after the government and our rip-off-artist lawyer took everything we owned.

My crazy aunt is well over six feet tall. OK. That's not quite true. I lie a lot since my father went to jail. (Or so my mother tells her friends on the phone when she thinks I'm not listening.) But she's *nearly* six feet, and she's so skinny that she looks like she might float away. She only wears one outfit: a muumuu and slippers. Muumuus are long dresses with long sleeves that are cut something like a painter's smock, except that they're sometimes made of silk. A muumuu is always pink or purple and always covered with flowers. My aunt has eight million. OK. Maybe not eight million. But no one could call me a liar if I said she had a thousand. It's a fact.

Her name is Mary. Aunt Mary. She's actually my mother's aunt, which makes her my great aunt. We didn't used to visit her much. She lived on the wrong side of the tracks. Now we live on the wrong side of the tracks with her, and we visit with her every day.

The one thing I like about Aunt Mary is that she doesn't nag me. In fact, she thinks whatever I do is "terrific" or "swell." I could spend the whole day eating onions and puking on her carpet and she'd think that was super. "Super," she says in response to almost anything I do. She's also a "fount of wisdom," as my mother says. For instance, one morning she told me that all a man needed to make it in this world is a hot lunch and shoes that can hold a shine. I told her I needed a motorcycle, because I was late for work and my boss was nuts. "Well, we'll have to find you a motorcycle then," she said. Then she kissed me on the head, which I can't avoid because she's so tall and quick that she always plants one on me before I know what's going on.

I think it made my Aunt Mary happy that we went broke and all crammed into her house. She certainly likes to kiss us.

4 Dad's trial took forever. Like, it took forever to even get started and then took forever for him to finally get sentenced. That's how they do it. First, they arrest you. Then they try you in court. Then they sentence you. They might have let my dad come home between the arrest and the sentencing, but they called him a flight risk. He wouldn't have been a flight risk if he hadn't tried to run. But try to run once, they think you'll try again. Apparently some of the lawyers for the government also thought that Dad had stashed money away somewhere. If he did, I never saw any of it. So he better not have. Anyway, the possibility that you've got some loot somewhere makes you even more of a flight risk.

That was one of the things Mom was most mad about—that Dad couldn't come home during the trial. "Why did you try to run?" she said over and over in the prison visiting room. "Where did you think you'd go? There were eight cops with guns."

He just kept saying, "I wasn't thinking clearly."

I was just as happy to have the guy out of our lives, given what he put us through. The only reason I occasionally wished he was around was so he could flip burgers instead of me. That was the first job I got after Dad got sentenced. First job I ever had. I didn't need to do it for more than one day to realize that I hated it.

A month before the sentencing was when we moved into Aunt Mary's. The jury found Dad guilty, so the jig was up. No more hoping it'd all blow over. Dad was in the slammer and there to stay. Probably for a few years, our rip-off-artist lawyer told us.

We had to put our house on the market and sell it for "way below what it was worth," my mom said. But we had to take what we could get. Couldn't wait around for the right price. The bill collectors were knocking.

We hired a bunch of cut-rate movers who broke things and weren't nice to my mother. When we first moved into our house eight years earlier, the movers were all in nice uniforms and kept calling me "tiger" and "big guy." These guys didn't say anything to me. They just grunted.

I guess it didn't matter too much. We had to sell most of our stuff anyway, so there wasn't that much to move. We just kept what we couldn't sell, and the things that had sentimental value. Let me say this about things with sentimental value: the only things I felt sentimental about were our pool and our big screen TV and the stereo I used to have that cost five thousand dollars.

"I bet you're the only kid in town with a five-thousand-dollar stereo," my dad said when he bought it for me.

It was true. And now I'm the only kid who had to sell his stereo to pay off his dad's legal bills.

The first night in Aunt Mary's house was kind of creepy. In

our old house there wasn't one speck of dust anywhere. Vacuum cleaners were built into the walls and cleaning people came three times a week to make everything spick-and-span. I wasn't crazy about having maids going through my room. But mostly they left me alone and didn't tell my mother if they found food under my bed. Once, I had an entire pizza under there. Upside down. I was sharing it with Frank when we knocked it over. I just kicked it under the bed. "Someone will get that later," I said. And I was right. The maid, Kirsten, told me that she didn't like seeing things like that, but that she wouldn't tell my mom. I liked Kirsten. I liked her cleaning my room, keeping everything spick-and-span.

Anyway, the first night in my new room at Aunt Mary's was hard. The whole place smelled like dust and mold, and my bed was nine million years old. It had something like a big ditch running down the middle, and was really lumpy. I think my great-uncle died in that bed. When I asked my mom if that was true, she told me not to be silly. But you can't tell with a place like Aunt Mary's. In my old house, a guest could be confident that he or she was getting a bed where absolutely no one had died. At Aunt Mary's, you had to take your chances. Who knows what could have happened in such an old, dusty place?

The one thing I liked about my room at Aunt Mary's was that I had a huge closet. It was actually more like another small room. And it had a lock, so I could go in there, lock the door, and feel comfortable that no one would bother me.

I started hiding out in the closet when my dad was sentenced. The judge gave him three and a half years. It's not that I was that upset. I wanted to write the judge to tell him to keep the guy in longer. Didn't want him coming back any time soon. But my mother was a wreck. I couldn't face her. And I didn't want her to see me. I guess I was a little upset. And every time I saw my mom it just made us both feel worse. So the closet seemed like the perfect solution. "Just perrrrrfect," as my aunt says.

5 Like I said, the first job I had when things went south was flipping burgers. I worked at a place called Fast Burger, which was a dump and a place I never would have even stepped in before my family went broke. There was only one good thing about my job: I was quitting. Just as soon as I could figure out how to pull it off. I wasn't the kind of man who could be held down for long.

"We have to get used to this," my mom kept saying.

I kept saying, "Not me. I'm not a man who can be held down for long."

The truth is that no one was really happy about me working at Fast Burger. The boss hated me and told me as much. And once school got out for the summer, it got even worse, because I started putting in more hours. My boss once yelled at me for fifteen minutes straight for what he called my terrible attitude. "So fire me," I thought. But he couldn't because Fast Burger was way understaffed.

He said, "All I'm asking is that you smile, be polite to customers, and get their food in a timely manner. Every time someone orders a burger and fries, you act like you're being insulted."

"The customers here are rude," I said. "They act like I'm their slave."

"They just want their food, Brett."

"They should learn some manners."

When I said that the boss nearly hit the roof. But he calmed down a bit before he started talking again.

"The only one who needs to learn manners is you," he said. "You know we're in a pinch with employees. So it's no secret that it'd be hard for me to fire you right now. But you're starting to make me crazy. And I'd rather be shorthanded than put up with the kind of attitude you've been showing around here. So it's your choice. Behave or you're going to have to leave."

I wanted to get up and walk out. But I didn't. I thought about my mother and my sister and about how flat broke I was. So I didn't. But I was going to. Couldn't take it anymore. Who did he think he was?

The thing is that I needed the money. Right before getting that fifteen-minute lecture, I had blown all my cash on a so-called luxury item. It was a luxury item then. But there was a time when my family wouldn't have thought twice about buying it.

Here's what happened.

My sister, Hannah, kind of thought she had a weight problem. Actually, I thought she looked great. But she was paranoid that she was fat. Maybe it's possible that she could have lost a few pounds. It's possible. But she was definitely not fat. In my opinion, at least. Anyway, seeing that summer was starting, Hannah needed a new bathing suit. She was in eighth grade and grew like twelve feet that year. My mother got a discount at the department store where she had just started working. She told Hannah to come in and pick out a suit.

I was at the department store as well, wandering around, checking out things like expensive sweaters and leather jackets. Eventually, I went to see how things were going with my sister. When I got to the women's swimsuit area, I saw my sister crying. She wasn't screaming crying. She was just softly crying. My mom looked sad too. But she was trying to be tough. That's a look she developed during the trial—the tough look. I asked Hannah what was up, and she said that all the suits made her look fat. She said the only one that made her look halfway decent cost two hundred bucks. That's right. Two hundred bucks.

The thing is that my sister has never been a snob about clothing. Never. She's never cared about expensive clothes. She was just feeling bad about the way she looked, and she thought that the way the two hundred dollar bathing suit was cut made her look better. Whatever. The point is that my sister's a real trouper. A real team player. So she didn't complain when my mother said that there was no way we could afford the suit. She cried, but only over the way she thought she looked. She didn't complain about not getting the bathing suit. She just kept saying that she felt like she looked awful. It really hurt to hear that. No joke. It was really hard to see her feeling so bad about herself.

Anyway, I was paid at Fast Burger two days later. And with that paycheck and some money I had saved up, I bought the bathing suit for my sister. I thought my mom would be mad, but she wasn't. When she found out, she just shook her head and said that I was going to get myself in trouble if I spent my money that way. But my sister was really happy. So happy she started crying again. How about that?

Anyway, I say all this to point out that I'm actually a very kindhearted guy. Not like my boss said—a spoiled kid with a lot of attitude. I'm sweet and good-natured. All the way through.

6 One of the worst things about my dad getting nailed by the law was that the prison they sent him to was in a place called Hartsville, which was pretty far away. Five hours, in fact. Just to see Dad. The jailbird. Of course, when the state government of California once talked about building a jail three towns over, the whole city of Glenwood was furious. "We don't need a prison around here," everyone said. Even my dad. Who knew that a new prison would have improved our life so much, would have been so convenient? We could have seen Dad every afternoon instead of just weekends. Wouldn't that have been great?

Actually, I didn't even see Dad every weekend. My mom did, but she said it was a lot to ask a teenager to ride five hours there and five hours back every weekend. Damn right. I didn't need to spend every weekend with my jailbird dad.

This is going to sound cruel. But it's true, so I'll say it. (If there's one thing my dad's behavior has taught me, it's to always tell the truth.) One of the things I liked to do when I first started visiting my dad was to be a wiseass. You know why? Because he was in jail and there wasn't a thing he could do to me. It was kind of like every kid's dream. I could say things like, "Hey Dad, you're a loser and an idiot," and he'd be sitting behind a big Plexiglas window and couldn't do anything.

My mom got mad. She mostly got mad on the car ride home. She'd tell me that my dad loved me and that we needed to stick together—no matter what happened. I usually responded with another wiseass comment like, "Uh, Mom, are you trying to tell me Dad isn't a loser, because last time I checked, which was this afternoon, it looked like he was a loser to me."

My mom never knew what to say to comments like that. And that's usually when I felt guilty. When my mom had a lot to say, it meant she was just bossing me around and acting like a mother. When she had nothing to say, especially about my cruel comments, it meant that she was really upset. I upset her a lot. I always felt bad when I did. Really. I loved my mom and hated to see her upset. But that never stopped me from making my obnoxious comments. You can't help being who you are. I am a wiseass. A wiseass by nature.

Anyway, Dad deserved everything he got. I may sound like a spoiled rich kid who's mad at his dad because he lost all his money, but there are actually solid psychological reasons for me to hate my dad. It's like what the school psychologist told my mother: when a father gets sent to jail, it's like he's betrayed the trust of his children. It's like Dad didn't care about us enough to make sure he stayed out of jail. That's the official reason I had to hate my father. But I usually denied it. When the school psychologist talked to me, I told her that I was just pissed off because we lost all our money. And I wasn't just saying that to be obnoxious. It was the truth. At least in part.

7Let me tell you about my best friend, Frank. There's lots of stuff he doesn't know. I can't be too hard on him. When I was in his position, I didn't know any of it either. But I'm a quick learner. Frank is a slow learner.

For instance, toward the end of the semester, right after I started my job at Fast Burger, he and I went to see a movie. It seems crazy, but putting together ten bucks for a ticket actually took some work. My mom gave me a couple of bucks. My aunt gave me fifty cents, which was actually helpful. And I had to fork over the rest from my paycheck. I'd never dreamed that scraping together a lousy ten bucks would be hard. But with all the expensive swimsuits I was buying, every dollar seemed kind of important.

Anyway, when we got to the movie theater, we ran into some friends. They wanted to sit with us, and they wanted to buy Cokes and candy and like a million buckets of popcorn. I managed to get away with throwing in only a buck. No one really said anything, but I think it's mostly because no one noticed. Money flows easily with them, like it used to with me. And who would ever think of weaseling out of a few bucks for popcorn? I'd think of it now. But they wouldn't. Wouldn't even cross their minds.

So that was kind of difficult. But after the movie it got worse. Everyone wanted to head over to Lauribelle's, a pretty cool restaurant where kids in my school like to hang out. At this point I was flat broke, and while I didn't mind eating someone else's popcorn, I didn't think it would be a good idea to order a burger and a shake and hope no one would notice when I didn't pay. I told Frank I didn't want to go.

"Let's head back to your house, Frank," I said. "I don't really feel like Lauribelle's tonight."

"What are you talking about?" Frank said. "You love Lauribelle's. There's going to be ladies there. Like . . . *ahem* . . . Nicole."

Nicole was a girl I had a crush on. Had it for years. Whenever I figured out her whereabouts, I was there. In less than ten minutes. Always. So when Frank told me she'd be at Lauribelle's, I really wanted to go. But wants have nothing to do with anything. That's what my mom said over and over when we first lost our money. "There are lots of things we want that we can't have," she'd say. "You need to accept that. You should have learned that lesson even when we had money. I'm sorry you have to learn it now."

"It's just such a terrible thing to know," I always replied. "I wish I never knew what a horrible place the world was."

Anyway, I wasn't going to Lauribelle's, but I still wanted to hang out. "C'mon, Frank," I said, still standing outside the movie theater. "Let's go back to your house. What do I need to go and ogle Nicole for?"

"Ogling Nicole is the only thing you like to do."

"Not anymore. My ogling days are over. Kaput. Finished. Nicole's ancient history."

Frank just stared at me for a minute as though I was speaking Russian. Finally, he said, "I don't want to go to my house. I want to go to Lauribelle's. If you want to come, great. If not, I'll see you tomorrow."

He said this smiling. Frank loved me. Idolized me. Worshiped the dirt beneath my feet. So, there's no use in calling him mean. But I wish he would have thought about my situation for a minute. He could have figured out why I didn't want to go to Lauribelle's if he thought about it. Just for a second. But he didn't. That's why I call him a slow learner. I learned all about being broke the first day our money ran out. It's an easy lesson to learn if it's you who's got nothing.

8 Of course, Frank's cluelessness had a sort of value. His lack of understanding meant he didn't treat me any different. For instance, it was kind of hard going to school after the news of my father broke. No one was mean. No one said anything to me. But I could tell that everyone knew what was up. In the halls kids were either overfriendly, or they gave me nervous looks, like I had to be the unhappiest guy in the world. One way or another it sucked. Everyone's behavior, good or not, just reminded me of what a joke my life was. Every time anyone said "hi," it was like they were saying "sucks to be you, dude."

Frank was different. His complete lack of understanding also meant that he didn't think it sucked to be me, or that he didn't think it sucked to be me any more than it had always sucked to be me.

When news of the Gerson disgrace first broke, my teachers acted like freaks as well. At the time that the front page article about my dad came out, we were studying labor unions and coal miners in my history class. My teacher, Mr. Philips, was pretty hard on people who made their fortunes off the sweat of other people's work. And good thing, too. Those guys were pretty evil. Anyway, he made lots of comments about how unfair the U.S. economy could be and how rich people always got away with everything. After the article about my dad appeared, he toned it all down. It was nice of him. It was nice that he didn't scream about crooked businessmen as much. But that kind of thing was painful in its own way. The fact that he didn't rant about crooked businessmen as much only meant that he thought my dad was one of them. And I guess he was right. My dad was a crooked businessman. Still, no point in laying off the crooks for my sake. As far as I'm concerned, crooked businessmen should go to jail. Send them to jail and throw away the key.

The one other thing that was weird was dealing with things like sports and homework. For instance, the job I had to get at Fast Burger kind of got in the way of my life. I managed to keep my grades up. Pretty much. Still, it sucked to have to plow through algebra after working all afternoon.

And then there was my brilliant athletic career. I always ran spring track. Kept me in shape for the fall soccer season. After I went broke, I had to juggle track practice with my job schedule. And contrary to what they say, track coaches and bosses don't have much sympathy for a young man's hectic schedule. "If there's one thing I believe in, it's sacrifice," my coach always said. He especially liked to say it when I told him I couldn't stay for the extra "captain's laps" that people ran after the official practice. See, there's a limit on how hard the coach could work us, so after the regular practice was over, there was a voluntary practice arranged by the captain. I never used to mind it. I actually liked working out, despite the fact that I'm a naturally lazy human being. But no way was I running "captain's laps" if I had to work at Fast Burger later on. There's a limit on what a man can be expected to do in this world. I believe in sacrifice too. Just like my coach. But I don't believe in torture, except in the case of crooked businessmen, of course.

9 I suppose my dad was never a bad dad. In fact, before he ruined my life, I'd say he was pretty good. I'd give him a B+. He didn't give me everything I wanted, which would have earned him an A. But he only yelled at me when I deserved it.

He didn't make me work too hard for my allowance. And he showed up to most of my baseball and basketball games. The one thing my dad wasn't was sentimental. He wasn't what you'd call a loving father. Some kids have dads who are always trying to hug them. My dad would pat me on the back, maybe even shake my hand. But there was no hugging. The other thing he didn't do was tell me he loved me. That's not to say he didn't love me. I'm pretty confident he did. He just didn't say it. He was a tough guy. A real businessman.

So get this. On one of my first trips to Hartsville Prison after I started my job at Fast Burger, my dad told me he loved me. He put his face close to the glass and said, "Brett. I want you to know something. I'm sorry all this happened. And I love you."

I thought about telling him that he was a loser and an idiot again. But I couldn't. In fact, I couldn't bring myself to say anything. I just stood up and walked out of the visiting room. That's another thing you can do when your dad's in jail. You can stand up and walk away from him while he's speaking to you. Can't do that if your dad's not behind bars. I was one lucky kid.

On the drive home, my mom gave me another lecture. Since the drive is five hours, she saved it till the end of the drive. You don't want to bawl someone out and then have to sit with them for five hours. Especially in our new car. We sold the other cars—the Mercedes, the Land Rover, and the red convertible my dad called his dream car, the Ferrari, which is Italian for "Poor People Can't Afford It." To replace our excellent cars, we got a small, simple Ford, which was economical and practical, and "not that bad," as my mom said. But it was too small to sit in for five hours with someone you were yelling at.

In general, my mom's another good parent. She'd get an A–, and she'd only get the minus as a matter of principle. No one gets a perfect A unless they do my bidding without question. Anyway, I don't have a mom who yells a lot. But she does give me lectures. I deserve them all. I listen to very few.

Anyway, one of my mom's key features, one of her assets, is that she's very pretty. Pretty in a mom sort of way. I think, at least. She has long straight blond hair—dark blond, not bleached. Her eyes are deep brown. And she has a kind of glimmer in her eye that makes you think that something exciting is about to happen. Actually, that's how she used to look. She mostly looks the same now. Except there's no glimmer. Or the glimmer comes and goes. It's always gone when she's lecturing me, especially on car rides back from seeing Dad. But it wasn't just an absence of the glimmer. It was the presence of a new look. It wasn't even a look of anger. It was the look of someone who's really tired. And that was a look I hated. It was a look that always made me sad.

My sister hated the look too, and because of the look, she

started lecturing me as well. But never in front of Mom. When we got back on the day that my dad told me he loved me, Hannah came into my room and knocked on the door of my closet. Normally I didn't allow that. But Hannah said she wasn't leaving until I opened up.

"What?" I said when I opened the door.

"You should be nicer to Dad," she said. The floor of my closet was covered with pillows and blankets and had a little set of shelves where I kept a radio and magazines and stuff. I sat back down on a pillow when Hannah started talking. She sat too. Most of the time I didn't allow that either. But I guess I was in the mood to talk.

"I can't be nicer," I said. "I hate him. How can I be nicer?"

"You don't hate him."

"I do hate him."

"You don't really hate him."

"No, I do really hate him. I really hate him."

Hannah sighed and rolled her eyes. "Do you love Mom?" she asked.

"Most of the time," I said.

"Then you should be nicer to Dad. It really upsets Mom when you're mean to him."

"We must each of us bear our burdens," I said, quoting Aunt Mary, who said that when I complained for the eight-millionth time about having to eat generic cereal. "We must each of us bear our burdens," I said again.

"I think," my sister said, "I think you should make it one of your burdens to be nicer to Dad."

"That, Hannah, is a burden I will not bear," I said. "Maybe I can manage to stop telling him that he's a failure and a loser and an idiot. But I'm not telling him I love him. No way. He's the man who sent me to Fast Burger. He's the man who took my swimming pool. He's the man who disgraced the good name of the Gerson family. Love must be earned, dear Hannah, and earned it he has not."

"OK, my wise sage," Hannah said. "Don't tell him you love him. But knock off the meanness for Mom's sake."

"I will consider your request," I said. "Now leave me for I must think in peace."

Hannah stood up and then leaned over and hugged me, which, let me tell you, was another first.

"What is with this family," I yelled, not hugging back. "All this talk of love and all this hugging is freaking me out."

Hannah smiled and patted me on the head. Then she left me to enjoy my closet alone.

10 Here's a short account of my struggle up the corporate ladder.

I had to work at Fast Burger one afternoon, but I had the morning off, so I decided to head over to Frank's house. As I was walking over there—which happened to be a long way, now that I was on the wrong side of the tracks—I bumped into a guy named Alfie Moore. He drove a school bus and used to drive me to grade school.

I also knew Alfie because he used to clean our swimming pool, which was kind of like his summer job. He did it all year long, really, because it was California and some pools were used all year. But summer's the big season, and since he didn't have to drive a school bus, he was always racing all over town cleaning pools.

Alfie was in his mid-seventies and looked it. But he was always running around at a million miles per hour, which didn't seem normal for an old guy. He had also had a couple of heart attacks and even heart surgery, which I knew because our pool got really dirty during those times. (Guess who was forced to clean it.) Anyway, Alfie never slowed down any. It was kind of hard to explain. He'd have a heart attack, be in bed for a month, and then one morning I'd wake up and see this old guy running around our pool.

Alfie was also kind of funny looking. His hair was white and never ever combed. He was kind of short and extremely tan. He had eyes that blinked about twenty times per second. And he had big thick glasses strapped to his face with an elastic band.

The other thing I should say about Alfie is that everyone seemed to like the guy a lot. I know I did, in a strange sort of way. He always remembered everyone's name, was always ready to talk your ear off about anything he could think of, and he was the best damned pool cleaner in the town of Glenwood. He was a lousy driver. Terrible. But he knew all the kids that rode his bus, and parents were fine with his lousy driving because when he drove the bus he went very, very slowly. Parents also liked him because if a kid missed the bus or was sick, he always knew. And if you needed your kid dropped off somewhere special, he'd make a detour. All you had to do was ask. Rich people like that sort of personal attention, and it was part of the reason everyone loved Alfie.

Anyway, I was headed to Frank's that morning, before I went to work at Fast Burger, when I ran into Alfie about two blocks from my old house. I waved but when he spotted me, he looked kind of surprised.

"I didn't expect to see you," he said. "I thought you moved to Hartsville."

"Nope. Just my dad," I said.

Alfie looked a little puzzled and then finally said, "Did your parents split up?"

Hmmm. You don't read the papers much, do you, I thought.

"I guess you could say that," I replied.

"Well," he said. "These things happen."

"Yes, they do."

"I cleaned the pool at your old house last week. It's looking pretty good. Where are you living now?"

"On Gleebe Road," I said, and then added, "On the other side of the tracks." (There are, by the way, railroad tracks that actually go through the middle of our town.)

"That's near me," he said.

I kind of smiled. Kind of made me happy for some reason. "Well, at least that's one good thing about where I live," I said.

Alfie nodded, unsure what to make of my statement. Then he asked, "What are you doing this summer?"

"This and that," I said. "I actually have a job."

Alfie's eyebrows rose when I said this, because kids from my neighborhood almost never had after-school and summer jobs.

"Where are you working?"

"At Fast Burger," I said.

"Like it?"

"Nope."

"Seems like a hard job. I hate that food."

"It is. And I do too."

"Well listen. I'm looking for an assistant this summer. Got a lot of pools to take care of. If you're looking for a new job, or if you know anyone who might be interested, let me know. I need someone ASAP."

"I don't think cleaning pools is my calling."

"Well let me know if you change your mind. It's not a bad job, as jobs go. It might beat frying hamburgers."

"Maybe you're right," I said, not really thinking he was right at all. "Thanks for the offer. If things at Fast Burger don't work out, I'll come find you."

"I live at 521 Sheridan Avenue. Just a few blocks from Gleebe. Swing by if you reconsider."

"Five-twenty-one," I said. "Got it." Then I said good-bye and headed to Frank's house where I spent the morning swimming, beating Frank at video games on a wide-screen TV, and dreaming about being rich again.

After my morning recreation, I headed to Fast Burger. I can tell you right now that there's nothing worse than spending the afternoon flipping burgers after you've spent the morning in luxury. The minute I stepped in that place, I felt sick to my stomach. And then I started feeling pissed off, especially because just a few hours earlier I had to listen to Frank yell at his mom about how unfair it was that he had to take tennis lessons that summer. *That boy has a lot to learn.*

Anyway, what happened at Fast Burger that afternoon is kind of important.

One of my coworkers was this kid I knew from school. He was going to be a sophomore at the high school that year, like I was. But we had never really been friends. No particular reason. I liked him well enough. We just weren't really friends. Anyway, his name was Keith. He was about five feet ten inches tall, had a chiseled jaw, blond hair, and a few freckles. The truth is that Keith was also a pretty nice guy. His problem, I discovered, was that he was kind of incompetent. And when incompetence is left unchecked, it can be very destructive.

Anyway, I was getting bored with flipping burgers and decided to take a break. It wasn't officially my break time. But when my body needs a break, it needs a break. How is my body supposed to know what time it is? So, I went outside to take a break. But before I did I said, "Hey Keith, keep an eye on these burgers that are frying. They need to be flipped in a few minutes."

Keith said "All right," even though he was a little distracted because he was working the register at the time.

Anyway, when I came back in, the burgers were burned and

my boss was cleaning them off the grill. I looked at Keith for a moment, who turned away, all guilty looking. Then the boss looked up at me and said, "What the hell is going on around here?"

"Don't look at me," I said. "Keith was supposed to keep an eye on them."

"But aren't *you* supposed to be cooking them?" my boss asked.

"Yes. Technically. But I told Keith to keep an eye on them."

"But why? It's not his job. It's yours."

"I know it is. But I told Keith to watch things for a few minutes."

"Why? Why did you ask Keith to do that?"

"Because I stepped outside."

"Why did you do that?"

"I needed to stretch my legs a bit. I needed some fresh air."

I thought my boss was going to pop a blood vessel when I said this. "Brett," he said, "I've said it before and I'll say it again: you have serious attitude problems. You are really one of the worst employees I've ever had." And as he said this, and as I watched the little blood veins pulsing in his forehead, I suddenly remembered the offer from Alfie. Although it seemed absolutely impossible that I would ever clean anyone's pool, I used the promise to give me the strength to tell my boss that I wasn't going to put up with any of his abuse anymore.

"I wasn't raised to be abused by people like you," I shouted. "I'm sick of this treatment. The burgers burned. So what? It's not like it's the end of the world. It's not even my fault. Everything here is stupid and everything sucks and I've had it with the whole fast food industry and I'm outta here, buddy. Outta here."

Then I ripped off my apron and pulled off my hat and looked at my boss and said, once again, "I'm outta here." And then I left. Walked right out.

As I walked home that afternoon, I wondered if I hadn't overreacted a bit. Perhaps I had. I also asked myself the following: if I wasn't raised to be abused by people like my boss, what was I raised for? Was I raised to be a spoiled rich kid? Definitely, I thought. And Fast Burger was no place for a spoiled rich kid. It was time to find Alfie and sign up as a pool cleaner. Yes, being a pool cleaner is no job for a spoiled rich kid either. But it suddenly seemed much better than flipping burgers.

11 I knew my mom was going to go nuts when she found out I quit Fast Burger, so I figured I'd better find Alfie first and secure my new job. Then I could go to my mom and say, "Mom, guess who landed a great new job? Your boy is really moving up in the world!" This seemed better than, "I quit my lame-ass job and now I'm dead."

I found Alfie pretty quickly. I actually forgot his exact address, but I remembered that it was somewhere on Sheridan. As I walked down the street a little uncertain how I'd find his house, I suddenly spotted the pool-cleaning van in his driveway: "ALFIE MOORE'S CUSTOM POOL CLEANERS" it said in fat, curling letters along the side. That was easy.

I rang the doorbell, but no one answered. So I rang again and then started knocking. Eventually Alfie came to the door. He was covered in dirt and looking kind of bleary eyed.

"Busy?" I said.

"A little," he replied, smiling. "Gardening."

"Listen. I'd like that job. Fast Burger is history."

Alfie paused for a second and then said. "OK. You've got it. But let's talk about this later. When I can think about it some more. About the terms."

"All right," I said.

"Can you start tomorrow? If you come by at eight, we can talk more about the job then."

"How about the day after tomorrow? I have a few things I need to take care of before I leap into another career."

Alfie nodded and smiled. "OK. Day after tomorrow. But make it seven. We'll make it a full day."

"OK," I said. "Seven it is."

"Seven," Alfie said again, nodding. Then we said farewell and I left Alfie to get back to covering himself with dirt, or whatever it was he was doing.

12 "Brett Gerson lands a new job," is how I expressed myself when I walked into Aunt Mary's kitchen and saw my mom.

"Really?" she said. "I just got off the phone with Mr. Johnson and it sounds to me like you lost a job."

"Why did you call Mr. Johnson?" I asked.

"I didn't call him. He called me. Do you know why?"

"Because he wanted to ruin my life?"

"He wanted to tell me that you were ruining his."

"The guy's a big jerk. He treated me like a slave."

"Brett. You have a lot to learn about the real world."

"I've learned enough, thank you, and don't want to know any more." My mom normally rolled her eyes when I said things like this, but this time she gritted her teeth and glared at me. She was clearly in no mood for my sarcasm.

"Sorry. Sorry," I said quickly. "But the thing is that I got a new job. I wouldn't have quit, but I got a new job. A much better job." At this point I smiled again, thinking that this announcement might defuse my mother's anger. But it didn't.

"That's not the point. I hear you burned five pounds of hamburger and then, instead of apologizing, you told Mr. Johnson that Fast Burger sucked. Is that how you put it? That Fast Burger sucked."

"It wasn't my fault. He went ballistic on me."

"It sounds like it was your fault to me."

"What did he say?"

"He said that you left five pounds of hamburgers frying while you took an unscheduled break. He said that you asked a kid who was busy on the register to keep an eye on the grill. He said that the burgers started burning a few minutes after you stepped outside. And he said that when you came back in, you started yelling at him, instead of apologizing."

I paused for a moment, thinking about the story. "That's right. It was the kid on the register who let the burgers burn."

My mom glared at me again and I could tell this argument was going nowhere.

"What?" I said.

"The bottom line is that it was your job to make sure the burgers got cooked and you failed. That's the bottom line."

"Has the whole world gone crazy?" I shouted.

Suddenly my mom took a step closer. "You have a lot to learn," she said.

I was going to restate my earlier point that I already knew far too much. But my mom looked pretty mad. So I decided that this might be a good time to keep my mouth shut. I decided to let her cool down and tell her about my new job later. I sighed, turned, and headed for my closet, where I was confident no mothers or lame-ass bosses would be lurking.

13 Not long after I locked myself in my closet, there was a knock at the door. It kind of pissed me off. A closed closet door indicates to most decent people that the person inside is busy. I'd never dream of knocking on someone else's closet.

"Go away," I said.

But the knocking continued. Just lightly. But it continued.

I figured it was my sister coming to check on me, and then decided it was my mother who had come to my closet to make up. My mom and me are pretty close. It may not seem like it. I'm a real wiseass to her. But we're still close. So when the knocking continued I opened the door, because, after all, I don't like fighting with my mom anymore than she does. But when I opened the door I discovered it wasn't my mom or my sister at all. It was my Aunt Mary. She had a bologna sandwich and a glass of milk.

"Here," she said. "Here's a bologna sandwich and a glass of milk."

"Thanks," I said. And I wasn't just saying "thanks" to be polite. I was actually pretty hungry.

"Burnt food is never anyone's fault," she said. I nodded, because I agreed with her and was happy that someone finally saw the situation from my point of view. "But when food burns," she continued, "it's always best to say you're sorry, even when it has nothing to do with you."

Hmmm. More homespun wisdom. I nodded again, even though I didn't really understand what she was talking about.

"Thanks for the sandwich," I said again. She leaned forward and kissed me on the head.

"You're welcome."

14 So about the time that I switched jobs, I came up with a brilliant plan to win the heart of Nicole, my true love. My real problem was just spending time with her. Since school had gotten out, I didn't get to see her as much. Perhaps I could have listened to the suggestions of my friends to call her up and ask her out on a date. But that's not my style. Or, I was afraid she'd say no. I needed to see her a bit more, impress her with my wit and personality. And let's face it, I was flat broke. Nicole was a quality woman. Couldn't just take her to the park.

Anyway, girls love parties. It's a well-known fact. So I talked Frank into having a pool party. Or, rather, I forced him into it. I came up with the idea because my birthday was approaching. Now, let me say that in no way did I want to have a birthday party, and I planned to keep my birthday and the pool party completely separate. The only thing I was looking forward to about my birthday was that I was going to finally get my driver's license. But that's how I came up with the idea of a party—just thinking about my birthday.

"This will be a great chance for me to hang with Nicole," I said, after I first made my proposal.

"I thought you were through ogling her," Frank said.

"I am," I replied. "Totally through. That's why I want you to have a party. I'm trying to take us to the next level. The post-ogling level."

"Why don't *you* have a party."

"At my Aunt Mary's? I don't think so."

"I think it would be fun. Your aunt could make us sandwiches and we could all dress up in her muumuus."

"Funny. Tell you what: if you throw a party, I'll let you hang with my aunt any time you want."

"I just don't feel like throwing a party. Too much effort. Too much work. Too much hosting. I hate being a host."

That was Frank for you. Social couch potato. If I had been back in my huge house, I'd have been throwing parties every day. Just goes to show that money is wasted on the rich. After being poor, I can see how true that is.

But there were reasons besides laziness for Frank's resistance. He also didn't want to socialize in front of his parents. I understand. It's not like I like kissing girls in front of my mom. I don't even like talking about them with her. Frank wanted to keep his family out of his social life. I know this is the case because he told me as much. After telling me that it would be too much work he said, "Anyway, no way do I want my parents spying on me while the whole school is running around my backyard. What if I want to make out with a woman?"

He had a point. But this is a tough world, and Frank had to learn to face his troubles. We were having a party at his house and I wasn't budging. I couldn't spend my whole life worrying about other people's problems. I also knew that I could very easily bypass Frank's stonewalling. Frank Ballard was not the person in charge of the Ballard household. The person in charge was Mrs. Ballard. And she loved me. Loved. And she also felt sorry for me. The poor boy who lost all his money and whose dad was a no-good jailbird. I always made a special point of eating everything I could in front of her: made me look hungry; emphasized my image of the poor boy; got me lots of sympathy and lots of invitations to do fun things.

Anyway, after Frank told me that he'd rather spend the rest of his life playing video games than help me win the heart of Nicole, I took the matter to the real powers that be.

"Hey, Mrs. Ballard," I said, walking into the kitchen, where Frank's mom was hanging out. "I think we should have a party."

Frank was close behind me. "No, no, no. Forget it," he said. "I don't want to have a party."

"Why not, Frank?" his mom said.

"Because I don't want to have a party."

"He's just being shy," I continued. "The reason we should have a party, Mrs. Ballard, is that I'm in love and I need a way to talk to this girl that I'm in love with."

I know, pretty sappy and definitely embarrassing. But you have to go with what works. I knew that no mother could resist that ploy.

"Awwwww," Mrs. Ballard said. "Let's start planning right away."

"No. No. No party. I absolutely refuse," Frank said.

"How about we just don't invite you," his mom said.

"No. No party at all."

"If I want to have a party, I'm going to have a party," Mrs. Ballard said. "If your friends happen to be invited, is that my fault?"

"No party," Frank said again. But now he was whining. He knew the argument was over. All mothers by nature love to play matchmaker. It's another fact that a man has to learn if he's going to get anywhere in life.

Anyway, I decided to make my exit at this point. Didn't

want Mrs. Ballard to change her mind. Once I left the house, her offer would become a promise. If she went back on her word, she'd have to disappoint a poor, fatherless boy.

"I've got to head home," I said. "Need to rest up. I start my new job tomorrow."

"Good for you," Mrs. Ballard said. "I think next summer Frank will be joining you in the workforce."

"Fat chance of that," Frank yelled.

"Frank!" his mother replied. "It's time for you to learn some responsibility." And with that, after so ably causing an argument between mother and son, I said farewell once again, and headed out the door.

15 My mother grew up without much money. Not that she was poor. She just didn't have a lot. Her father was a line worker in a factory in St. Louis, Missouri. She talked a lot about those days after my dad was first sent up the river. "I've been such a fool about so many things," she'd say. "I just got too swept up with money."

This shouldn't indicate in any way that my mom had regrets about staying with my father. Incredibly, she seemed to love him more than ever. She just kind of felt like she had gotten soft.

From my perspective, Mom was out of her mind. Have regrets about losing your money, not about losing the crook— that's what I always said.

Anyway, my mom's childhood in St. Louis was the topic of many of our discussions in the car when we visited Dad on weekends. My mom would talk about picnics in Missouri forests, trips to St. Louis parks, hikes along the Mississippi.

Mostly I'd respond by saying, "Mom, you're like boring me out of my mind."

When I'd say that, my mother usually just smiled and kept telling her boring stories. My traitor of a sister would usually chime in as well. She'd say, "I like hearing the stories." And that was it. I could never win that argument.

One weekend we were driving home from visiting my dad. The trip had been irritating, as usual. I didn't think I could take another minute of watching my dad whine about how much he missed us, and when my dad asked if I missed him I told him to "bite me." OK. That was pretty bad. Even I know that. Anyway, on the way home, my mother got particularly sentimental about her childhood. Talked nonstop about being poor and pulling together in times of trouble. She went on and on. Kept saying things like, "If there's one thing I learned when I was young, it's that life is very, very difficult. There are no easy answers." And, "Sometimes things don't work out the way we want them to. The important thing is to adjust. To learn."

Finally I took a deep breath and said, "Mom, I'd like to take this opportunity to point out that we are not where we are today because of fate and misfortune. We're here because Dad's an idiot and he blew it. He blew it for all of us. This is not the same thing as a poor family trying to make ends meet in times of hardship. Catastrophe did not happen to us. It was caused by Dad."

"Well," my mom said, pausing slightly. "I understand your point. Maybe I even think it's true. I think all I'm really trying to say is that life is very hard. And we all face hard decisions. And we don't always make the right choices. And we have to forgive each other when we mess up."

"Mom," I said.

"Yes," she replied.

"No way."

16 So anyway. The day after I quit my job, I did nothing but sleep and eat. The only variety in my day was where I slept and what I ate. I slept in my bed, on the couch in the TV room, and in my closet. I ate an entire box of cereal, a bologna sandwich, a gallon of milk, a pork chop, three potatoes, and exactly nineteen green beans. Had to have nourishment and rest to prepare for my big day.

I was ten minutes early when I showed up at Alfie's the next morning. He was sitting on his front stoop. "You're early, Brett," he said. "I like to see that."

"Don't get used to it," I said. "I'm almost always on time. But I'm almost never early."

"As long as you're on time, that suits me."

It was kind of funny, standing there with Alfie. When you know a guy as one thing your whole life, it's hard to get that image out of your mind. The thing I was mainly thinking about as I arrived on Alfie's stoop was what my dad used to say about him. Every time he saw Alfie he said, "Sheesh, that guy never gives up." It was a reference to his heart attacks and to his heart surgery and the fact that he was always running around like he was crazy. But it was also just a reference to the fact that he was old. Truthfully, it *was* kind of strange to see this old guy running

around your pool, cleaning out vents, scooping up dead squirrels, and measuring chlorine levels.

Of course Alfie had the last laugh. My dad always used Alfie
to explain a theory of his. He used to say, "Take a look at Alfie
Moore. Now there's a guy who works harder than anyone I
know. But what does he have to show for it? Not much. It's
important to do more than work hard. You have to know how to
work smart."

Profound words, Dad. You should have taken your own
advice.

Anyway, when I arrived, Alfie stood up and said, "Need
some coffee before we get started? I need another cup."

"Why not?" I said.

I followed Alfie into his house and through the hallway to
his kitchen. Everything in his house seemed to be a million years
old. But it was clean. That's for sure. No dust or dirt anywhere.

Alfie's kitchen seemed modern enough—for a bus driver.
The coolest thing about it was a huge set of shelves filled almost
entirely with preserved food. There were preserved peaches,
pears, onions, green beans, watermelon rinds, tomatoes, carrots,
and like a million other things. I didn't necessarily want to try any
of them. I prefer my onions fresh. Still, they looked pretty cool.

"How do you take it?" Alfie asked.

"Take what?" I said.

"Your coffee. What do you want in it?"

"Ummmmmm."

Did I mention I had never had coffee before? I don't think so. I'll say it now. I had never had coffee before. Not once. Always seemed pretty gross to me.

"I take it black," I said, trying to give my voice a tone of authority. "Always drink it black. Best that way."

I should have taken milk and sugar. In fact, I should have just asked for a glass of milk and skipped the coffee all together. It was terrible.

"This is terrible," I said after taking a sip.

"Don't like my coffee?" Alfie asked.

Time to come clean. "All right. I'll be honest because I don't want to insult you. Never had coffee before. And for the first time in my life I realize that my parents were doing something right when they denied me this evil drink. Coffee, let me say right now, is disgusting."

"I can't live without it," Alfie said. "C'mon, take another sip."

Because I was always a good sport about this sort of thing, I took another sip. "Still terrible," I said.

Alfie took the cup from me. "Don't worry about it. We'll try again tomorrow."

"I don't think so," I said.

"I'm going to make it part of your job to develop a taste for the stuff."

"Part of my job?" I said.

"Yeah. I'm your boss and I command you to like coffee."

"This is like Fast Burger," I said.

"It's going to be worse than Fast Burger," Alfie said and then smiled.

17 Worse than Fast Burger? Not quite. But you'd be surprised how tiring cleaning pools can be. What's worse, on a summer day, it's incredibly hot. Hotter than any other job. Know why? 'Cause you're not allowed to swim in the pools. How do you like that? You spend all sorts of time keeping pools clean and you're not even allowed to use them. That makes cleaning pools especially hot work.

Actually, I should point out that this was Alfie's rule, not the rule of the pool owners. I found this out right away.

At about seven-thirty, we arrived at the first pool we had to clean. It happened to belong to a family named the Harrisons. My family had known them for years. The kids were much older than me and my sister, but our parents were close, at least until my dad's criminal activities scared them off.

Anyway, I had swum in this pool a million times before, and when we arrived, I thought I'd jump in for a few minutes because I love to take a dip in the early morning. But when I took off my shirt, Alfie flashed me a funny look, like he couldn't figure out what I was doing. When I started walking toward the edge of the pool, he figured it out pretty quickly.

"No, no, no. No swimming in the customers' pools," he said.

"What?" I replied, confused.

"No swimming in the pools. They don't want strangers swimming around in their pools."

"I'm not a stranger. I practically grew up in this pool."

"Doesn't matter. Today you're a pool cleaner and you can't go in."

I half thought that Alfie was joking, but he gave me a look that indicated he was serious. I again tried to comprehend all this. Was I really not allowed to swim in the Harrisons' pool? Alfie kept giving me his serious look.

"OK," I said. "No swimming in the customers' pools."

If I was with my boss from Fast Burger, I would have jumped right in. But I guess Alfie was different. It was hard for me to be a wiseass around him.

As I put my shirt back on, I thought about how I would have

reacted if I woke up one morning and saw Alfie swimming around in our pool. It seemed like kind of a funny image to me, but I didn't have too long to think about it because I was quickly given my first instructions.

As Alfie opened his tech bag and prepared to test the chlorine levels, he said, "Why don't you grab the net and start by getting those leaves off the bottom of the deep end."

"You got it," I said. I walked over to the net and began my career as a pool cleaner.

Now let me tell you one more thing. It will save time, because this fact about my summer didn't change. Cleaning pools is humiliating. Sure, Fast Burger was humiliating. But in a different way. Basically, you have to be a humble human being to eat at Fast Burger. So when I was humbled, I was humbled before the humble. What did I care if some Fast Burger–eating freak saw me making his lunch? Now I was serving the rich. Not that that mattered much to me, except that I used to be one of them and they all knew me. I actually didn't think it was going to bother me that much. Then Mrs. Harrison came out to say hi.

"Brett Gerson?" she said. "Is that you?"

"Hi, Mrs. Harrison."

"What are you doing here?"

"Cleaning your pool."

"Cleaning my pool?" she said, as though it was some kind of outlandish prank.

"With Alfie. I'm working for Alfie."

She kind of looked surprised. But then she quickly smiled, because rich people like to pretend that they're not snobs and that no one's beneath them. Take it from me because I was once rich, rich people think all sorts of work is beneath them. It's not a mean-spirited snobbery. Everyone loved Alfie. They all thought he was diligent and lovable—deserved nothing but praise. And rich people are all in favor of hard work. In any given conversation I ever had with rich adults around Glenwood, I always got lectured about the benefits of hard work. But ask one of those people, those people like Mrs. Harrison, if their kids were going to be cleaning other people's pools and they'd look at you like you were out of your mind. They wouldn't laugh or be angry. They'd just look at you like you had asked if they thought their kids lived on Mars.

Anyway, Mrs. Harrison smiled and said, "Is this your summer job?"

"Yes. Pool cleaner," I replied.

"Well," she said. "That is exciting."

"Yes, ma'am. Very exciting."

Mrs. Harrison smiled again, turned around, and headed back into her house.

I'll get more specific about similar events later, including the day that I first cleaned the pool at my old house. That was crazy. But just bear in mind that Mrs. Harrison's idiotic behavior was pretty much what I got out of everybody. The truth is, I could kind of take it. Fine, I was humiliated. But it beat flipping burgers. And there are not many opportunities these days for a man who's only got a freshman's level of education. I was a humble working stiff. Like Tom Joad in *The Grapes of Wrath*. I was having my own miniature Great Depression right in the middle of Glenwood, California.

18 So cleaning pools makes a man hungry. Especially a man like me, a man who loves to eat. So when noon rolled around on my first day, I was pretty happy that Alfie suggested we break for lunch. In fact, I was ecstatic. I was extremely hungry.

We had cleaned three pools that morning. Sucked up all the leaves, scooped away all the bugs, carted off the dead animals, and made sure the water was safe—all for the rich people. Working for the rich makes a man hungry. Did I already say that?

We went to a luncheonette called Fitz's. That's another place I never would have gone before the Gerson family went belly-up. But I have to say that I was missing out. I got a huge cheese-burger and a plate of fries and it was truly one of the best meals I've ever had because, like, I was starving. And Alfie picked up the tab, which he told me he was going to do when the waitress showed up.

"This won't be regular," he said, after we ordered. "Nor-mally, you should pack a lunch. But since this is the first day, and all. Well, what the heck. It's on me."

"Sounds good to me," I said.

"We should also talk a bit about what you'll be making and how much you'll be working. I think I'm going to need you about forty hours a week. I assume that's fine."

"OK," I said, thinking that there was no way I could get through forty hours a week.

"What did you make at Fast Burger?" he asked.

"Five-fifty an hour."

"I'll give you eight. But you've got to keep my schedule."

"For eight, I can keep your schedule."

"It'll be a lot of early mornings."

"I can get up. I love to sleep. There's no question about that. But I can get up that early. I'll just nap when I get home."

"That shouldn't be hard to do. If we start at seven, you'll get home around three-thirty."

"I can live with that," I said, smiling.

After lunch, Alfie and I drove to the next pool. I know I've said it before, but I'll say it again: Alfie was the very worst driver I've ever seen. His driving strategies in the van, however, were completely different from his driving strategies in the bus. In the bus, he may have driven like a lunatic, but at least he drove like an insanely slow lunatic who was well aware that he was carting around a bunch of kids. In the van he drove like nothing mattered in the world, especially not me. He drove way too fast, he never read any signs, and if you were to, say, scream your head off like you were going to die, he wouldn't even notice.

I saw it a little that morning. But Alfie was still sleepy then—despite all the coffee. But after lunch, after he was fortified by a thick hamburger, there was no stopping him. I am not exaggerating when I say we very nearly killed a million people.

My dad used to laugh about Alfie's driving—another thing he made fun of Alfie for. When Alfie was coming to clean the pool he'd say, "Everyone stay inside today. Alfie's coming."

For all the crazy things my dad ever said, that was solid advice.

Anyway, we cleaned four more pools that afternoon. When

he dropped me off, it was four o'clock. I was exhausted. And my nerves were shot—from his terrible driving.

"Seven again tomorrow?" he said, as I was getting out of the van.

"OK," I said. "Seven again tomorrow."

"Don't look so glum. It's four o'clock. You can take a nice long nap."

"Nap?" I said. "I don't think so. I think I'm done for the night. Time for bed. Like right now."

Alfie laughed as I shut the door, and then drove off. Very funny. The man sees he's very nearly worked me to death and he laughs as he drives off. Very funny.

19 All right. Let me sketch out the time frame here. It hasn't been too clear. Dad gets his face busted in the kitchen in October. We were broke by March and Dad was convicted in April. In mid-May, I became a burger flipper, about a month before school ended. End of June, I quit that lame-ass job and ditched my dumb-ass boss. Beginning of July, there I was, a pool cleaner.

So July second was my first day of work. That was a Wednesday. I worked Thursday, which was the third—cleaned seven pools, just like the day before, only no free lunch. And that Friday I had off, because it was the Fourth of July, and I'm a patriot, and patriots take Independence Day off.

In Glenwood, they have a big fireworks display over a place called Tillman's Lake. I can live without fireworks. What I can't live without is the socializing that goes along with them. Since school was out, I didn't get to see Nicole every day, and I was looking forward to heading down to Tillman's Lake with Frank and scoping out girls.

We got there in the early afternoon. Some friends of ours had dragged a grill down to the lake and were planning on cooking out.

Just to give you the big picture, let me describe a few of the key players in my larger group of friends. Frank was my best friend. I've already described him: a lovable but occasionally obnoxious guy who spent much of his life in confusion but whom I could trust, if I really, really forced him to be trustworthy.

Then there was Josh Esperillo, whose dad owned a company that made yogurt. Now, yogurt is something I hate, but, apparently, enough people like it to have made Mr. Esperillo a gazillionaire. He was a yogurt baron.

There was Tim Regis, who had huge muscles and curly blond hair and was kind of like our front man when we were trying to meet women. If we were a rock band, he would have been our lead singer. Unfortunately, none of us were at all musical—I say unfortunately because girls love musicians. That's a fact. Anyway, Tim's dad also happens to be a judge, and he talked to my mother quite a bit when she was figuring out just how screwed we were.

There was Tony Brightman, who was generally pretty cool, except he was a little wimpy, which made him a less likely lead singer than Tim. Tony would have made an excellent bass player. No one was quite sure what Mr. Brightman did, other than make a lot of money. He had "businesses here and there" that included restaurants, video stores, dry cleaners, that sort of thing. He just owned a lot of things and watched the bucks roll in.

And then there was a guy named Monster, who had always been called that for no good reason, and who was in fact a very timid, skinny kid who was good at tennis and video games. Monster's dad was a computer programmer and made a fortune off the Internet.

There were others, I guess, but those were the guys I was closest to.

Anyway, Nicole was part of a group of girls who sometimes

hung with Frank and me and the other guys we spent our time with. But whether or not she would choose to hang with us was hit or miss. It depended on what Nicole's options were. Occasionally a group of older guys who played sports and were pretty buff would invite them to do something. If that happened, we were ditched. No questions asked. And we didn't really complain. It was the law of the jungle when it came to boy–girl interaction. If a group of older guys claimed our girls, what could we do? We'd just try to hang out with another group of girls until Nicole and her friends came back to us. It's the unfortunate truth. But I tell it like it is. I am a straight shooter.

Anyway, when Frank and I arrived at Tillman's Lake there was, like, not a babe in sight.

"I thought you told me you invited Beth," I said. (Beth was Nicole's best friend. They were inseparable.)

"I did," Frank said. "She said that she'd talk it over with Nicole and that they'd think about it."

"This is why you're throwing a party," I told Frank.

"I'm not having a party."

"Fine. This is why your mom and I are throwing a party. Nicole will definitely be there. You can ask a lady like that to come to an upscale pool party. But you can't ask a woman like Nicole to eat burgers from a grill. She's a white-tablecloth woman."

And then suddenly there she was. Nicole. With Beth and the

rest of her group of friends, walking toward us. Nicole was in shorts and a loose-fitting T-shirt and tan and all summery looking. It would have been my lucky day. Really. I really would have been thrilled. Except that right behind her was the group of older guys that poached on our babes—the law-of-the-jungle babe poachers. How convenient. We were all in the same spot. Maybe we could all be friends. Maybe we could all hang out together.

Nope. The babes and the dudes walked right past us and down the beach to set up their own grill, and the girls acted like we had never even invited them to join us.

They were nice, the girls and the older dudes. They weren't mean. The older dudes liked us. "Wussup Brett," they all said to me as they walked away with the love of my life. See. No hard feelings. They thought I was cool. But they had claimed Nicole and her entourage for the Fourth. Nothing to discuss. It was the way of the world.

The girls said hi to me too, and Nicole even waved and smiled. "Hi, Brett," she said, in that diabolical way that she tells me hi that makes me act like an idiot because it's just so clear how much I love her.

"Hi, Nicole," I said.

And that was it. She just kept right on walking, leaving us

younger and second-rate guys standing next to a grill with way too much food.

But I need to say something again. A lot of guys would have called Nicole stuck up. And maybe she was, a bit. But she was a good person. She just happened to be beautiful and had a million guys after her. What did I expect? And I could take the disappointment because deep down I believed that one day she would be mine.

"No way will that girl ever go out with you, no way," Frank said, passing me a jar of olives.

"Thanks, Frank," I said. "We'll see."

20 My mother tried to make visits to see Dad voluntary. In other words, she tried to let us decide whether or not to go. But if the visits were completely voluntary, I never would have gone. Not once. My sister would have. She still had warm feelings for the old man. But not me. Visits were always under duress.

Anyway, that Saturday morning we took off for Hartsville.

My mother wanted to spend the Fourth there, but I put my foot down. She said, "Fine. We'll compromise. We'll wait until Saturday the fifth, but you had better be nice."

The compromise was that I went at all. Good behavior was a bonus gift. I wasn't promising anything. The only thing I was happy about was that the crappy hotel we normally stayed in had a crappy pool, and after cleaning pools on Wednesday and Thursday, which seemed to last for like a hundred years, let me tell you, I was excited by the idea of actually getting to swim in one myself.

The car ride to Hartsville took forever. The roads were full of stupid drivers and our cheap-ass economy car makes five hours feel like fifty. The AC doesn't work right, and my mom kept it low to save on gas, and because things didn't go so well with me and Nicole the day before, I was pissed off the entire time.

"I've got an idea of how to economize," I said.

"How?" my mother replied, quickly glancing away from the road and smiling at me.

"Let's stop visiting Dad. We'll save a fortune on hotels and gas."

"Please don't start this again," she said.

"I'm not starting anything," I replied.

My mother sighed and bit her lip, and I felt guilty. But I didn't say anything to make her feel better. Not my policy.

When we got to the hotel, I decided to take a dip before we went to see my dad. My mother said that it was out of the question. I said it was out of the question that we go see Dad before I cooled off. Again my mom told me that I was not to go swimming. I just put on my bathing suit, walked out of the dinky hotel room that I always had to share with my mother and my sister, and dove in. The whole time my mom was screaming, "Don't go in that pool. Don't go in that pool."

Like that's going to stop me.

So I went swimming. Only for ten minutes. But when I got out of the water, my mother and sister were gone. Big deal, I thought. I just kept swimming, and after an hour or so, I went back to the hotel room. I plopped down on the bed, turned on the TV, and watched a movie.

After about five hours of swimming and TV watching, my sister and mother finally came back.

"Where ya been?" I said as they walked in the door.

My mother and sister just looked at me.

"We're tired," my sister said.

"What are we going to eat? I'm starved."

"We already had dinner," my mother replied.

"Did you bring me anything?"

"Nope. We figured you could take care of yourself."

Interesting development.

"OK." I said, "I guess I can. Looks like fried chicken for Brett."

I rolled off the bed, put on my shoes, and opened the door.

"Be back later," I yelled.

"Brett, wait," my mother said. I could tell that she suddenly felt bad that she didn't bring me dinner. Feeding kids dinner is one of the things mothers need to do to feel good about themselves.

"Yes?" I said.

"I don't want you gone long."

I didn't respond.

"I want you back in half an hour," she continued. "The chicken place is right across the street. There's no reason for you to be gone very long."

Again, I didn't say anything.

Then my mother reached into her purse and pulled out five bucks. "Here," she said.

"It's OK." I said. "I've got cash. I'm a working man, remember?"

"Take it. Don't be silly."

"No prob, Mom. Really. I'll get it."

"Brett, take the money."

I stepped out the door and shut it behind me. It kind of hurt not to take the five bucks. But I had to be firm. Still, I returned to the hotel in about half an hour. No reason to be overly difficult.

Usually parenting happens by coercion, blind obedience, and love. The coercion comes when your parents bully you into something. They say, "No allowance unless you clean your room."

Obedience comes in when you do something simply because your parents tell you to. They might say, "Go outside and see if the paper is here," and you do it for no other reason than that they told you to do it.

Love comes in when you do something because you want to make your parents happy. Like, you could probably get away with not giving your mother a Mother's Day present. But you get one for her because you love her. You might even clean out the garage because you love her. You might do it even though there's no threat, no payment, and no direct order. You might just do it because you love her.

When your dad gets thrown in jail, coercion, obedience, and love fly out the window. You realize that the whole parents-boss/kids-slave rule is just an illusion. You make your own money, so the coercion thing stops. You drop the obedience thing because why would you do something just because your lying, cheating dad tells you to do it. And the love thing. Well, I loved my mom. But my love had kind of changed. I didn't feel the same kind of dependence that I used to—like, a pet dog might love you because it needs you to survive. When your parents let you down, you realize that you don't really need them to survive. Sometimes, they even seem to threaten your survival. Maybe you still love them. But it's in a different way. You don't really need them anymore. To survive, that is.

But let me say one thing so I'm perfectly clear: I did not love my father.

21 So the next morning, we went to see Dad. I went along without putting up a fight. I had made my point the day before. I could relax, now that I had taken a stand. When we arrived it was the same old thing. Dad sitting behind a Plexiglas divider with little holes in it. The three of us asking dopey questions from the other side. There were other families there too, each in their little cubicle, everyone looking sad. Everyone except me.

After we chitchatted for a while—about weather, food, Aunt Mary, my job with Alfie—my dad suddenly looked at my mom and my sister and said, "I think I need to speak to Brett alone for a few minutes."

Great, I thought. More "I love yous." I'm not saying it, I

thought. No way. But when my sister and my mother got up and left and it was just me and my dad, I discovered that my dad didn't have that kind of conversation on his mind. In fact, he was kind of pissed off, if you can believe that.

"Brett, why do you have to give your mother such a hard time?"

"Why did you have to steal money?" I responded.

"I didn't steal. It didn't work that way. But that's not the point. We're talking about you. Why do you have to give your mother such a hard time?"

"Why does she have to give me such a hard time? We get along fine when we're not dealing with you."

"Brett. I know that I might not be in the position to ask you for anything."

"That's right."

"But I'm going to anyway. And it's simple. I want you to act more like an adult."

"Like you? An adult like you? You want me to commit crimes, 'cause that's what my role models do."

"No. I want you to accept that life is not perfect, that people are not perfect, and that there are all sorts of things in the world that disappoint us."

"You think I haven't accepted that?"

"No, I don't."

"Well, I have. I've gotten pretty used to the fact that my dad's a crook and that he blew it and that my life sucks."

"Look. I know you've had to face a lot. And I'm not asking you to do anything for me. But when I say I want you to be more of an adult, what I mean is that I don't want you taking out your problems on other people. I know it's tough for you. And I don't think I'll ever be able to make up for the things that I've done to you. But you've got to stop hurting your mom. You want to be a jerk to me, I'll live with it. I probably don't deserve any better. But your mom does. And I know you know she does. And I know you know what a good person she is and that she'll probably just take your abuse without saying too much about it. But just because I've hurt you, doesn't mean you should hurt her."

My father paused for a second to see if what he said had sunk in.

Finally, I spoke. "Dad," I said.

"Yes."

"You're an idiot."

I said this and stood up and saw his disappointed face and walked out of the visiting room because you can say and do that sort of thing when your dad's behind Plexiglas.

And he was speechless. In past times, he might have tried to call me back. This time I think he was too surprised and hurt. And it felt good to hurt him like that. It was a great feeling.

Great, except that suddenly and for no good reason whatsoever, I was also crying—like a baby, like it hurt me to say that to Dad. Kind of embarrassing, really. I tried to compose myself after I left the visiting room. Didn't want anyone to see me. But I was pretty upset.

I know. He was right. Dad's a smart guy. A real thinker. And as I stood outside the visiting room, I decided I would make an effort not to be such a jerk to my mom. I'd try to behave, even when it meant having to see Dad. But I wasn't about to act like I was doing this because Dad told me to. I didn't do anything he told me to. It was my new mode of behavior, my new personal code of conduct. Never do what Dad says. Still, I decided to be nice to Mom.

The car ride home that evening was pretty grim. Obviously Dad told my mother what I had said and I felt kind of bad because she must have been thinking I didn't care about her either. I did. But I didn't really know what to say. I guess I just figured that things would be different, that I'd act different. She'd see that I was nicer to her. Still, I wasn't going to act like Dad's speech influenced me at all. Couldn't have *that*.

22 Monday morning, bright and early, back to the swimming pool grind. I was at Alfie's at seven on the dot, although I was a little tired from the long drive back. Alfie was drinking coffee on his front steps as I approached.

"Good weekend?" Alfie asked.

"Best weekend ever," I said.

"Ready to do some work?"

"Yup."

"Coffee?"

"Not today, thanks. I'll start working on that assignment tomorrow."

"OK. I'll let you off the hook this morning. Since it's Monday."

After Alfie poured himself another cup of coffee, we jumped into his van and headed across town, across town to the other side of the tracks. I decided that part of the reason Alfie was such a bad driver was because of all the distractions in the van. With his coffee and the morning radio and Alfie trying to talk to me, I'm surprised he had any brain space left to focus on the road. And he was, after all, like a billion years old. Whatever. Clearly I'm alive to tell the tales of Alfie's driving. But the fact that I'm alive is purely a matter of luck. Nothing else.

Anyway. We cleaned pools that day, just as we did for the

rest of the week. By Thursday, I was completely bored. The only thing I really liked was eating lunch with Alfie. He told great stories, and he'd always let me sample his lunch.

We always ate under a big oak in Bryce Park, which is near where all the lousy pool-owning rich people live. Alfie's lunches were works of art. He said they were just leftovers, but they were clearly leftovers of tremendous feasts. Not once did he ever bring a sandwich. It was always some kind of Turkish stuffed vegetable or an African stew or a Malaysian salad. Drove me crazy, frankly, but when he shared his lunch, I was always surprised by how much I liked it. I'd say something like, "Hey Alfie, what the hell are you eating?"

He'd say something like, "This is tabbouleh." (Or *taziki* or teriyaki or Tetrazzini.) "It's great. Try some."

I'd say, "No way."

He'd say, " C'mon. Don't be a baby."

I'd say, "No way" again.

He'd say, "You're being a baby" again.

I always made him call me a baby at least three times. Then I'd try it. But only after putting up my little protest, just for fun. And it was always great. Then I'd say something like, "Right again, Alfie. You're a genius." And he'd smile and maybe dish some more of the food out into whatever Tupperware bowl or plate I was using.

Me, I always brought a sandwich. And it was either bologna or peanut butter. That's it. Sure, I could have done with more variety. But who could be bothered? Variety means work, and, as is well known, I hate work.

Anyway, we cleaned pools all week. And it was all the same. Until Thursday. I knew it was coming. But I forced it out of my mind. Even Alfie seemed to want to avoid the job. But when Thursday rolled around, it had to be done. Had to be done every week. Missed last week because Alfie had switched the schedule. But this week, no way out.

"I'm sorry about this," Alfie said, as we parked in front of my old house.

"No problem," I said. "I knew it was coming."

"Sad?"

"Not really. I hate swimming pools and this house. Most of all, it reminds me of my stupid father."

"Your dad's still in Hartsville, right?"

"Yep."

"Miss him?"

"Nope."

"What does he do there?"

I looked at him. I figured he would have known by now. How could this guy be so out of the loop?

"He's a jailbird," I said.

"What?"

"Don't you read the papers? He's in jail. The big house. The hoosegow. I'd figure the pool guy would know more gossip." Alfie just looked at me, and then I felt bad because he suddenly looked like he felt really guilty.

"I'm sorry, Brett. I didn't know. I should have. I guess I don't read the papers enough."

"Don't worry about it," I said. I reached over to open my door, but I paused. "It's not that big of a deal," I continued. "Suits me just fine, not having my father around." And then, for no reason at all, I just started telling Alfie about everything that happened. And I didn't give him the short version, either. I gave him the long one, complete with cops, bloody kitchen floors, and rip-off-artist lawyers. I told him how much I hated being broke and how my life used to be great and how my dad didn't care enough about me to make sure he stayed out of the slammer. And I went on and on. Like an idiot. I explained how hard my mother had it, how no bathing suits fit my sister right, and how my dad was a total jerk. "Like, the biggest jerk you've ever seen," I said. Then I paused. "Really. Absolutely the biggest."

Alfie just sat silently, holding the steering wheel as he listened. He gave me these hurt, sympathetic looks, like he wanted to give me some advice or apologize again. But he stayed quiet. What could he say? Not much you can say to console a kid whose dad is in jail. Still, Alfie was a good guy to talk to. I don't really know why. Anyway. After more stupid talk, we finally got out of the van and faced my house.

Believe it or not, cleaning the pool that day was a bigger pain in my ass than I imagined. Why? For a lot of reasons. First, we did it right before lunch, which is always the worst pool to clean because it's midday and boiling out and you're absolutely starving, and you know you still have a hot afternoon ahead of you.

Then there were all "the memories," which is a phrase I put in quotation marks to indicate that it's a stupid phrase that I hate. Sure, it was strange to be there. I grew up there after all. But by the time I moved out, I had gotten over my nostalgia and was ready to get out. Yeah, memories came back. But I can't say I wasn't happy to be out of the place.

The strangest event happened when Mrs. Alder, the owner of the house, came out to chat. The thing is that I had met her before. Twice. The first time was when she came to look at the place. She spent about three hours walking around, asking my mother questions, some about the house, others about why we were moving. My mother said as little as possible, and Mrs. Alder was too stupid to know that she was venturing into sensitive territory.

The other time I met her was at the closing of the sale, when Mrs. Alder and the real estate agents came over to swap the deeds and the cash. Actually, there was no cash at all. I always figured if we sold our house, someone would show up with a big suitcase full of cash.

"It doesn't work that way," my mom told me. "And anyway, all this money goes to the people we owe, especially Dad's lawyer." Our rip-off-artist lawyer always scammed a huge cut. What a joke.

Anyway, I met Mrs. Alder at the closing as well. I shook her hand, she told me I was a handsome young man. I smiled. And that was it. But we still met. That's why I was surprised when she didn't recognize me. But stranger and more insulting was how she did refer to me. She came galloping out of the French doors that opened onto the patio singing, "Oh, pool boy. Poooool boy. Poooool boy."

No joke. Pool boy. She called me pool boy.

"Are you talking to me, Mrs. Alder?" I asked, feigning politeness.

"Are you cleaning my pool?" she said.

"Yes."

"Then I'm talking to you."

I wanted to tell her that my name was Brett Gerson and if she called me pool boy again I'd deck her. But I was suddenly completely embarrassed, and decided I was much happier if she didn't know who I was. I had been embarrassed for the whole week. But now I really felt like a loser. This used to be my house after all. Now I was cleaning the pool.

"What can I do for you?" I said after a slight pause.

"I was wondering if that other fellow was about. The older gentleman?"

"Alfie?"

"Yes. Alfie. We're having guests next week so I'd like to get the pool cleaned again in about four days. Do you think that will be a problem?"

Suddenly Alfie appeared carrying a long net and his tech bag.

"Hello, Mrs. Alder."

"Hello . . . Alfie," she said. "I was wondering if I could get you to come early next week as well."

I took the net as Mrs. Alder and Alfie sorted out the next visit and started scooping leaves. It was funny. A year ago, I never thought my dad would be in jail, my mom would be working in a department store, and we'd be living with Aunt Mary. But I really never thought I'd be cleaning our pool as a hired servant and that some bitch would be calling me pool boy. What a joke. My life was a joke.

23 Alfie knew it was tough on me to clean that pool, so we did it in record time. We had lunch that day under the oak in Bryce Park and Alfie gave me a piece of baklava, which is a Turkish pastry with nuts and honey in it. Delicious. I knew it would be too. But I still complained and said the food looked gross, just like I always did.

In the afternoon we cleaned Frank's pool. That was a chore I was expecting. Cleaning my old pool was too horrifying to think about; I knew it was coming, but I couldn't think about it. Cleaning Frank's pool was only mildly horrifying, so I could actually dread it without too much psychological damage.

The reason I knew about it was because Frank's mom had told me two days before. Normally, Frank's family used someone else to clean their pool—a "corporate outfit," as Alfie called it because it had ten employees. When Frank's mother found out where I was working, she changed services. She thought it was a favor to have me clean her pool. Some favor. But I did get some praise from Alfie.

"Bringing in new business already," he said, after getting a call from Frank's mom. "Not bad. I think I'll keep you."

When Alfie and I showed up, Frank was at the tennis lessons he hated so much. But his younger sister was there to gawk at me as I walked around her pool cleaning out the dirt and the dead things.

Frank's mom came out several times to tell me and Alfie hello and to ask if we needed anything. She also told me again that Frank was going to be working next summer. "I think it will be good for him," she said. I think she believed it too. But I knew it wouldn't happen. Kids in that neighborhood never worked during the summer. It's not that they were lazy. It's just that they were too busy enriching themselves. They took tennis lessons, went to computer camp, studied for the SATs, went camping in Oregon, that sort of thing. Fine, Frank's mom was a great mom, and I knew that she liked me, and I didn't mind doing menial labor for her. But if she wanted Frank to have a job, it would mean that he couldn't have some kind of fabulous learning experience. And I knew Frank would play that card. He may hate tennis lessons, but he'd take classes in flower arranging before he'd get a job. I almost said this to Frank's mom but I just smiled.

"Frank's going to love working," I said. "Just like I do."

As Alfie and I were finishing up, Frank's mother came out once more and invited me to dinner the next day—that's Friday, in case you've lost track. Frank's mom is a great cook, and seeing that she loves me and all, how could I refuse?

"We'll be grilling steaks," she said. "I thought we could plan out our exciting party then as well."

"I'll be here. Right after work," I replied.

24 So Friday was an easy day. That was the way Alfie liked to work it. Throw in a few extra pools during the week and finish early on Friday.

"Got to start working on my garden on Friday afternoon, or the whole thing falls apart," he said.

"I need to start relaxing on Friday afternoon, or I start falling apart," I replied.

Alfie dropped me off at my house at about one-thirty. Aunt Mary was watching soap operas when I got home.

"How was your day?" she said, as I walked in.

"Great. Just like always."

"Are you hungry? I could make you a sandwich."

"I'm fine," I said. "Alfie and I had a quick bite before we cleaned our last pool."

"Well you just let me know if you want a sandwich," she

said. And then I heard the television changing channels. It's a testament to how much my Aunt Mary loves me that she would have interrupted her soap operas to make a sandwich. She tries to watch two at once, flipping between them. There's something kind of strange about that. It's also kind of impressive. It's hard to keep track of two shows at once. I've tried.

Anyway, I went up to my closet for a little leisure. I would have watched TV, but obviously it was being used. So I slept instead. If you can't watch TV, the next best thing is sleeping. Actually, if you're rich, TV is only one of many great distractions. First, you probably have more than one TV. And along with TV there's swimming in the pool, going out to eat, and buying expensive things. That sort of stuff is fun too. But if you're a poor man like me, you have to nap in your closet. A closet with pillows is like a poor man's swimming pool.

After my nap I decided to head over to Frank's house for dinner. It was about four-thirty. Early. But I knew that Frank's mom would have plenty of food ready for my arrival, and that it might be fun to actually swim in their pool for a while rather than clean it. We also had to talk about the party.

Frank was still at tennis lessons when I arrived. Frank's mom was already setting out huge bowls of chips and dip and plates of cheese and that kind of thing. I asked if I could swim for a little while, before I started eating. She gave me a look like

I was out of my mind to ever ask her permission. "Of course," she said. "You can do whatever you want."

I'm actually starting to feel bad about the way I describe Frank's mom versus the way I describe my own mom. They're actually a lot alike. But my mom had a lot on her mind (obviously) and it was harder for her to spend time having barbeques, planning parties, and feeding friends. She normally loved to do that kind of stuff, but these were not normal times, I guess.

I was also a billion times nicer to Frank's mom than my own, which made me feel bad as well. But my mom was my mom. I guess that's just the way people act to family members. Snotty and spoiled. Frank, for instance, was no different. His mom spent all day doing things to make him happy and he acted like she was a complete idiot. It's a hard thing to explain.

Anyway, after swimming for about half an hour, I went into Frank's kitchen and started chowing on his mom's food.

"So when do you want to have the party?" Frank's mom said.

"It doesn't bother me," I said. "Whatever works for you. I've got to visit my dad next weekend."

"How about two weekends after that," she said, picking up a calendar and looking at dates in early August. "Saturday looks good."

"That seems fine to me."

Just then Frank walked in the door, carrying two outrageously expensive tennis rackets and looking really sweaty. He looked at his mom and me studying the calendar and said, "We're not having a party."

"No, you're not having a party," his mom said. "We are."

"You guys can't be serious," he said, stomping his feet like a two-year-old. "You're not really going to throw a party, are you?"

"We're serious all right," I said. "You'd better get used to it. You can either join the fun, or let it pass you by."

"Mom. He's only doing it to get a girl."

"I know exactly why he's doing it. What better reason to have a party than to get a girl?"

"This has to be a joke," Frank said. He plopped his rackets on the kitchen table, took off his shirt, walked out back, and jumped in the pool.

"He'll come around," I said.

25 So that night we had a huge dinner of steaks and asparagus and baked potatoes. Frank's father cooked the steaks, as men in my old neighborhood like to do, and he asked me how everything was going. He was a friend of my dad's, and had even been to visit him in jail. That was something. Most of my dad's friends ran like hell when he got sent to the big house—probably because they were crooks too and didn't want to get busted. But Frank's dad was all right. Even asked me how my dad was doing, rather than pretending that my dad wasn't a crook.

Mrs. Ballard and I tried to talk more about the party, but when she asked what kind of food I wanted Frank interrupted.

"Look," he said. "This party is against my will. But I'm willing to deal with it, since I seem to have no choice. All I ask is that no planning be done in my presence. If you promise me that, I won't complain anymore."

"It's a deal," Frank's mom said, happy that Frank was now resigned to the party. "We don't want your input, anyway."

"You're just going to have to trust us to invite the girls you have crushes on," I said.

"I can't wait to find out who they are," Mrs. Ballard added.

"I can't believe this," Frank said, as his father and sister laughed.

I headed home right after we ate. I was exhausted. I slept like a baby that night, and didn't wake up until noon the next day. I was a working man, after all, and needed rest. I didn't even notice the huge ditch running down the middle of my bed. Slept right over it and didn't even notice.

My mom was in Hartsville for the weekend, so Saturday and Sunday passed without incident and plenty of sleeping. Aunt Mary made bologna sandwiches for lunch and dinner, and my sister tried to tell me how to live my life.

The only unusual thing that happened was that on Sunday afternoon my aunt decided to ride her bike to the nearby ice-cream shop. She wanted to make it a family outing but my sister and I said no way.

"I thought you kids liked ice cream," she said. We did. That was true. But we also hated being seen with old relatives who wore nothing but muumuus and slippers. And the hatred of embarrassment far outweighed the love of ice cream.

Of course, my aunt's attempts at being freewheeling and independent were grossly hindered by the fact that her bike was like eighty billion years old and had two flat tires and a seat that looked like it was made out of leaves and vomit—not joking about that either; the leather was totally rotting.

Anyway, no sooner had my aunt left the house, telling us that we would miss all the fun, when she came back in to ask me to help her pump up her wheels.

"You've got strong arms," she said. "Let's put them to work."

I followed her out to her ancient garage, found the pump,

and blew up the wheels. I asked my aunt twice if she was sure she wanted to do this. She just said, "Of course. Why do you keep asking me that?"

"Fine," I replied. "Have fun."

She said she would, and jumped on the bike and took off, way faster than she should have been going.

She came back about an hour later. She said that she was still upset that we didn't want to come with her, but that she decided to bring us back sundaes anyway.

"Not that you deserve them," she said. "I just wanted you to have them."

I should actually point out that we weren't really such needy, fair-weather relatives. We used to hang out with my aunt some before we went broke. Not a lot. There's only so much fun you can have with an aunt. Still we saw her every so often.

Aunt Mary was actually a pretty cool person when she was younger. I guess she was always a cool person, but when she was young she was cool in the way that only young people can be cool—cool in the way people are before they get old and become automatically uncool, if that makes sense. She was a nurse and traveled all around the world helping out people suffering from one kind of disaster or another. I've seen pictures of her in just about every spot on the planet. She looked like a completely different person. Young, happy, energetic. I guess she's happy and energetic now, although she's definitely not young. The main difference besides her age was that she dressed like a total freak, although as far as I can tell everyone did before I was born. Strange hair, weird clothes, everything you'd expect from people who were around back then.

She settled in Glenwood about thirty years before we went to live with her. "I just got tired of all that traveling," she told me one day over bologna sandwiches. "Too much damn moving around."

"Nothing worse than working hard," I said.

"Of course, I was also in love," she added. "With your great-uncle Henry."

My great-uncle Henry died about five years after my Aunt Mary moved to Glenwood. Apparently he fell out of the back of a pickup truck. This is what my aunt always said. She always kind of chuckled about it, although according to my mom Aunt Mary was totally brokenhearted when it first happened. My mom said her mother had to come out and take care of her for three months. I guess my Aunt Mary got over it. Or it just became another story to tell about my Great-uncle Henry. When I was living with her, my aunt would say things like, "Crazy guy fell out of the back of a pickup truck. What a character." But I know my aunt thought of Uncle Henry a lot. His picture was everywhere. I bet the ladies liked him. He was a pretty smooth-looking guy.

My mom met Uncle Henry when she was young, but she doesn't really remember him. She was pretty close with Aunt Mary when she was growing up—after Henry died. Aunt Mary was actually the reason we moved to Glenwood. My dad's job back before I was born relocated him to California. Glenwood seemed as good a town as anywhere to set up shop, and I guess the fact that my Aunt Mary lived there made my mom pretty happy. Of course, I would have preferred it if she lived in someplace like Hawaii, because that's where we could have gone after we lost all our money.

Another thing about her was that she was pretty cool about all of us moving in with her. I can pretty much assure you that if a bunch of family members showed up at my door, I'd think twice about letting them shack up with me. But my aunt was pretty relaxed. Nothing really upset her. She just smiled and rolled her eyes at various household mishaps, my numerous obnoxious comments, and even the fact that her husband Henry died by falling out of a pickup truck. Everything just slid right off her back. She was as cool as a cucumber.

And her coolness helped me out a few times. Once I called my math teacher a "dickwad" because he was asking me all these algebra questions that I, like, totally did not want to answer. I kept saying, "I don't know," and he kept asking me new questions. It was really aggravating. Finally I just looked up at him and said, "Can we give it a rest now, dickwad?"

The principal wasn't too happy with me. He kept asking me why I felt it was necessary to call Mr. Brinkley a dickwad. I wanted to say that I called him that because that's how he was acting. But getting sent to the principal's office was kind of freaky. It was a first for me. I decided I better not make things worse. I just told him the story he already knew, how I was a poor unloved boy whose dad was a convict. No adult can stay mad at you after you tell them that one. Still, I got suspended for a day.

When the principal called my house, my aunt answered the phone. She said that she was in charge and that she'd be down to pick me up. She came in, signed all the forms, and took me home—on foot, of course, because she doesn't drive. The walk was about fifteen minutes and I can tell you I wasn't looking forward to it. I was kind of embarrassed really. Who wants to get yelled at by an old relative? But she was really cool. She didn't say anything except, "Brett, I'm going to say this once and then as far as I'm concerned the matter is over: do not call other people dickwads." She didn't even tell my mom. That's kind of rare. Adults have a pretty tight conspiracy where they tell each other everything. Not my aunt. She was no stool pigeon. She knew how to keep her mouth shut.

My aunt's easygoing ways actually help to account for my sister's good nature. Without familial origins to explain it, my sister's behavior would be completely bizarre. My dad could have gone crazy and set fire to her hair, and my sister would have forgiven him. And she wouldn't have had to force herself to forgive him. She would have forgiven him just because forgiving is her thing. After all, she forgave him for losing all our money. Not much worse than that.

I suppose there are times when my sister got upset. Like when she couldn't have the bathing suit that her darling brother finally bought for her. And she was upset when things like horse-riding lessons and ski trips became too expensive for us. But she always got over it. Like in a day. Not me. I always make a point of letting things burn and fester.

To tell the truth, my sister's good behavior made everyone more worried about her than me. Expressing your emotions is very healthy. That's what doctors say. That's why I never hold back when I'm pissed off. When I'm pissed off, I tell everyone. But my sister never really said anything. They even sent her to a therapist at school because she didn't seem to be at all angry about the Gerson family's tragic hardship. No one could figure out how she could be so mature. Everyone was waiting for her to snap. No one waited for me to snap. I snapped right away and kept on snapping. Anyway, my sister didn't snap because she's probably the most kind and decent person there is. (Next to my aunt.) And I'm not just saying that because she's my sister. Frankly, it freaks me out. But it's the truth. My sister is one even-keeled person. One even-keeled and truly gentle and nice person. Of course, who knows how my sister will turn out? Maybe she'll be a total freak or an arsonist or a crook, like my father. Hard to say. But judging by how cool she is now, I think she'll probably do all right.

26 Anyway, my mom got back Sunday night. She said that Dad was fine, but a little depressed.

"He wanted to see you two," she said.

"Well, I wanted to spend the whole day driving around in our Mercedes," I replied. "Instead I had to rest up so I could clean pools all week. You think I care about Dad's problems?"

My mom was getting used to my wiseass comments. She barely even rolled her eyes anymore.

"Next weekend, right?" she said.

"I'll think about it."

"You already agreed."

"Then why are you asking me?"

"Because I love you," she said, grabbing me. "You're a brat but I love you anyway."

I squirmed out of her headlock. "Geeze," I said. "Everyone around here is completely nuts." But I kind of needed that hug. Hate to say it. But I did.

"Don't ever hug me again," I said. But I kind of smiled and my mom just laughed.

27 Monday morning I was up at six-thirty. One of the nice things about living on the wrong side of the tracks was that I was close to Alfie. I could roll out of bed, scarf a bowl of cereal, and be on his stoop with time to spare. I had promised Alfie I'd try another cup of coffee that morning, so I grabbed a pack of mint gum off the dresser in my mom's room on my way out, and, for no reason at all, I ran all the way to his house.

Alfie was sitting on his stoop drinking his hundredth cup of coffee.

"Ready to try some coffee again?" he asked.

"Lead the way," I replied.

Alfie got me a big mug out of the cabinet and told me he had used top quality Kenyan beans that morning. Whatever that means. As Alfie was pouring my coffee, I looked around the kitchen and noticed big piles of cucumbers everywhere.

"What's with the cucumbers?" I said.

"Making pickles," he said, handing me my coffee, which looked like slightly dark milk.

"Pickles for your trophy shelves," I said, pointing at all the preserved fruits and vegetables on the shelves of his kitchen wall.

"For the trophy shelves," he said. "But I usually eat most of these cucumbers right away. Before they make it up there. How's the coffee?"

I put the coffee to my lips. This time it was milky and sweet and more like a warm milkshake than that swill I had the first time. "It's not bad," I said. "Not bad."

Anyway, that was the start of my week, although the days that followed seemed pretty much the same. Early to rise, milky coffee with Alfie, a few wiseass comments about his latest cooking project, and off to the pools. That's one of the things about having a job—the things you do seem to repeat themselves. Over and over, day after day. So let me briefly summarize what happened that week:

Mrs. Alder called me pool boy again.

Frank's mother and I talked a little about the party.

Alfie made me drink more coffee.

Frank and I wandered around downtown, hoping to run into Nicole.

My mom yelled at me, and I yelled at her.

Alfie drove like a lunatic.

Aunt Mary made me sandwiches.

My sister scolded me for not being kind enough.

I rehearsed possible ways to declare my love to Nicole.

I tried to sleep as much as possible.

Only one really cool thing happened that week. Alfie and I were talking at lunch on Wednesday, just after we cleaned the pool at my old house. We were sitting under our usual oak tree in Bryce Park. I mentioned that I was turning sixteen in a few weeks and that I would be getting my driver's license, which, quite frankly, I was positive was going to be the greatest thing that ever happened to me.

"I got no wheels of my own," I said. "But Mom will let me borrow the car. My crook of a dad always said he'd buy me a car. But I guess that's out of the question now."

Alfie kind of looked at me and smiled. "You're kind of hard on the old man, aren't you?"

"Yep. I'm very hard on him. And he deserves it."

Alfie thought about this for a moment. "I guess he does," he said. "But there's probably going to be a time in your life when you wish you hadn't been so hard."

"Alfie."

"Yes."

"There will never be such a time. I promise you."

Alfie smiled, and then changed the subject. "Well, you're getting your driver's license. That's exciting. Sometimes I still get a kick out of driving."

"Some might say you enjoy it too much."

"I think everyone says that. But I don't care." Alfie paused and then asked, "Do you even know how to drive? I hear you have to know how before you get your license."

"No prob. I'm an expert," I said, although this wasn't quite true. "We had driver's ed at school."

"Been out practicing at all?"

"A little. With my mother. When she has time. I have a learner's permit. But I need an adult. To supervise me. Cause I might go crazy and run someone over."

Alfie stared at the oak for a moment and then said, "Tell you what. After we get done today, if you're not too tired, I'll let you take the van out for a whirl. If you think it'll help you get ready for your test."

"Great," I said, because that's actually how I felt. The van was a beat-up old piece of junk. But I still wanted to drive it. "Let's get going. Eat your lunch."

"All right, all right. But you better do a good job this afternoon."

"No problem. I'll do the best job you've ever seen."

Alfie smiled at me and then took a big bite of whatever the strange thing was that he brought for lunch.

28 So that afternoon I got to drive the van. As righteous wheels go, this van was not righteous at all. Not a bit. And it definitely wasn't a babe magnet. But I didn't expect to be cruising for babes with a seventy-five-year-old man in the car anyway. I took the van for what it was. A vehicle. And vehicles are fun to drive, especially when you don't have your license yet.

We started in the parking lot of a church, which was good because it was empty and also because I needed some divine help to drive Alfie's beat-up ride. As for safety, we were fine. After driving with Alfie, everything seemed safe. And one of the good things about Alfie's behind-the-wheel recklessness is that doing things like speeding around in tight circles in the church parking lot didn't bother him much.

"My mom would go nuts if I did this," I said, as we were speeding around in tight circles in the church parking lot.

"Not me," Alfie said. "Nothing scares me."

On that note of encouragement, I did about ten more circles and then headed toward the traffic. Now, I will remind you that the day ends for Alfie and me a little before rush hour. So traffic wasn't terrible. But around four in the afternoon in California, pretty much all traffic is bad. And so it wasn't like I could just peel out into the street without looking. Still, that's exactly what I did. Didn't even turn my head. Why? I don't know. I forgot, I guess.

"Brett?"

"Yes, Alfie?"

"In situations where you're pulling into traffic, it's always best to look."

"Really?"

"Yes. Did you see that car you almost hit?"

"No. There was a car?"

"There were several cars. Now. I'm not scared driving with you. Not one bit. I've seen much worse. But I'd hate to see your license revoked before you even get it." It was hard for me to pay attention to what Alfie was saying because I was having such a blast. But he kept talking. "I suggest you pull into that parking lot up there so we can practice a little more."

"You're scared, aren't you?"

"No."

"Scaaaared."

"Breeetttt." I almost drove past the parking lot. But I kind of knew when to stop with Alfie. He was a good sport. The best. He was always like that as a bus driver. He'd take all sorts of razzing. But you liked him, so you didn't really want to push him too hard. Same as when I was driving the van. I liked to tease Alfie as much as he liked to tease me. But I also knew when to pull over.

"Satisfied?" I said as we came to a halt, now in the mostly empty parking lot of a movie theater.

"Yes. Now let's try to do a few maneuvers that law-abiding citizens might use when they're on the road. And I recommend you obey the law because the Man will take your license if he ever gets the chance. I've seen it. He'll do it."

"Fine," I said. "Fine. What's my first instruction?"

We spent the next hour making turns, coming to full stops, practicing driving slowly, and I even tried parallel parking, which is nearly impossible in a van. After that, Alfie agreed to let me out on the road again. And he gave me new instructions about every three minutes. I did pretty well. Drove slow. Obeyed the laws. I even stopped to let pedestrians cross, although I told Alfie that after I got my license I was never doing that again.

At about five-thirty, Alfie and I were pretty beat. We drove toward our side of town and I parked in front of my house.

"Congratulations," he said. "You did pretty well. Maybe we can take her out for a spin on Sunday afternoon."

At first this idea seemed exciting to me. But I stopped just short of agreeing. "Can't," I said. "I promised my mom I'd go with her to see my crook of a father."

"I see. Well, you don't want to miss that."

"No. I do want to miss that. But I can't."

"I was right about what I said earlier, you know."

"About what?"

"That you're too hard on your father."

"I'm not hard enough. But I've been too hard on my mom. That's why I'm going."

Alfie paused and then smiled. "Well. I guess I'll see you tomorrow," he said. Then we both opened our doors. I headed toward my house as Alfie got into the driver's seat and took off.

29

That weekend, my father seemed to be acting a bit strange. In fact, he seemed to be completely out of his mind. I think the whirlwind of events was finally over, and he was settling down to realize that he was in jail. There used to be fighting, complaining, and the settling of financial affairs to keep him occupied. Now it was time for Dad to live his new life, which was really no life at all.

My dad wasn't a selfish guy, really. He was just an idiot. And I assure you he punishes himself every day for being an idiot. He's sorry for what he put us through. So sorry. Sorry to the point of apologizing every chance he gets. But by that point in the summer, I think he was mostly feeling sorry for himself. During that visit, he didn't apologize as much. He didn't ask as many questions about what we were doing. He mostly asked us to describe things. He'd say, "Tell me what Tillman's Lake was like on the Fourth," or "What did the old house look like when you cleaned the pool? Did it look good?" Funny, I hated the man more when he was concerned about me. Now that he was realizing that he was in the slammer, I felt a little bit of pity for the guy. Pity. Not love. Don't get me wrong. My dad's an idiot and deserves what he got. But it's just sad, I guess.

Let me tell you what my dad did. It's not like he shot someone, although the guys working for the government sure thought what he did was bad.

Basically, he cheated. It would be the same thing as looking at someone's cards while playing poker. Part of the rules of poker say you're not allowed to know what's in the other guy's hand. And if you do know, even if you just happened to get a quick peek, you've broken the rules. OK. If that happens and you're with your buddies, maybe they yell at you or even kick you out of the game for a while. But if you're playing serious poker, like with thousands (or millions) of dollars on the table, then that little peek is a different story. It can mean the difference between walking away broke and walking away a wealthy man.

So Dad was a stockbroker, and as I understand it (and as Dad has basically admitted) he broke the rules of being a stockbroker a bunch of times. He found out things he wasn't supposed to, and made a lot of money by buying and selling stocks based on that information. He also seemed to have a problem paying his taxes, although his rip-off-artist lawyer kept saying those charges were "trumped up and bogus." He didn't say that about the things my dad did to buy and sell stocks. For those charges he kept saying, "We can beat this rap." That is, the charges against my father weren't false or bogus, they were something that had to be beaten.

Apparently my dad's rip-off-artist lawyer did pretty well.

That's what he says. Dad could have gotten twenty years, or that's what our rip-off-artist lawyer told my mother when she called him about his bill: "He could have had twenty years, Mrs. Gerson. Twenty years. That's a long time. I assure you that we did very well."

Anyway, I think at that point in the summer, my dad was realizing just how long three and a half years is. That's a long time. This is what he said to me that weekend. He said, "Brett, I'm going to miss your high school graduation," and then he burst into tears. I didn't tell him he was a jerk and a loser. That was my way of being nice. But I also didn't tell him that it was all right and that I loved him. Nope. Wasn't going to do that. Wasn't going to let my guard down. You let your guard down, and they nail you. I wasn't getting nailed. No way.

30 So after that weekend, it was back to the pool-cleaning grind. Alfie was actually a pretty easy guy to work with. He wasn't always entirely alert—he was, after all, in his mid-seventies—but his confusion was always kind of funny. I loved watching him look around for bottles of chlorine or his tech bag, which he always seemed to lose. As time went by, I made a point of keeping track of those things. That was a bad move. Why? Because you do your boss a favor and the next thing you know it's your job. Remember that. Never volunteer for anything, because before you know it, you'll be doing the same thing all the time. Anyway, Alfie was always losing his stuff and then asking me to find it. I was the head tech-bag finder on our crew.

Alfie took me out to lunch again that week. On Wednesday. He even let me drive to Fitz's Luncheonette and parallel park. It's a good thing that I'm a freewheeling and easygoing kind of guy. Otherwise, I never would never have been able to park the van. There were like a million people beeping their horns at me to hurry up. But I wasn't intimidated. Nope. I took my time and did the job right. I'm a perfectionist. I wanted to make sure the pool van was perfectly parked.

Alfie was a sport too. He just kept saying things like, "Don't pay any attention to all those horn honkers. I never do."

Lunch was great. Alfie and I both got the meat-loaf special, which is a pile of ground meat, mashed potatoes, gravy, onions, and a couple of green beans. Just the ticket for working men like us.

We talked about a bunch of things. I was kind of planning out my strategy for the party at Frank's house.

"But you just said you've never even been on a date with her."

"Don't need a date to know that it's true love."

"I'm not sure you've got that right, Brett. I'd at least wait until after you spend a few hours with her before deciding you're in love."

"True love, Alfie. True love. True true love."

Alfie smiled, and then, for no apparent reason said, "I hope you were nice to your father this weekend."

Suddenly my meat loaf tasted like sawdust. What the hell was with all this father sympathy, I wanted to know. It was ruining my lunch. "Of course I was nice to him," I said. "As nice as I get to a man who ruined my life."

I think Alfie felt bad that he had hit this sensitive nerve, my oh-so-sensitive I-hate-my-father nerve. In fact, it looked like Alfie was going to apologize. But instead he said, "You know, I have a daughter. A daughter named Linda."

"I figured you must have children somewhere," I said.

"She pretty much spent her whole life hating me."

I kind of paused and then said, "What did you do?"

Alfie smiled at this—I think he thought it was funny how quickly I placed the blame on him.

"I did something bad," he said. "I left my wife—her mother—and moved to Alaska. Deserted them. It was bad. I paid my child support. Sent her birthday presents. As absent fathers go, I wasn't the worst offender. But things like child support and birthday presents don't count for much when you leave your family."

"Why did you leave?"

"I guess I wasn't much of a family man. That's not much of an excuse, I suppose. I got married when I was too young and couldn't handle it anymore. Fine. Rotten. I shouldn't have walked out. But I did. And my daughter never quite forgave me."

Alfie paused. "My wife was a little different. I drove her crazy, and when I left I think she was mostly relieved. She wanted something a little more stable and she remarried about a year after I headed north. Great guy. I ran into them once, back in California, and they seemed very happy."

"Did you see your daughter much after that?"

"Some. She loved it when I visited, but hated it when I went away again. Hated me for always going away."

"Does she live around here?"

"No. Portland, Oregon. She's a lawyer up there. Does pretty well. She moved there when she got married, before she got her own divorce. That kind of helped things between us. It was a rough divorce. But it taught her that life doesn't always go the way you want it to." Alfie paused for a moment, took a sip of his water, and then continued. "But I'm not sure that she's ever quite forgiven me."

"Alfie," I said.

"Yes."

"I don't think I can ever forgive my father."

"Maybe you can't." Alfie took a sip of his coffee. "But you should at least know that his mistakes don't have anything to do with how he feels about you. He should have been more responsible. But my sense from you is that you pretty much liked all the money he was pulling in. I'm not saying he was crooked for your benefit. But I think you should understand that a person can hurt someone else while still loving them. I'm not making excuses. I'm just stating a fact. Life is difficult and most of us do terrible things to each other. But that doesn't remove the good things we do for each other."

I thought about this for a second and then took a bite of my meat loaf. "Alfie," I said, "my dad's an idiot. I would have preferred that he had a regular job than get rich and lose everything. I can't forgive him. Even if I forgave him, he'd still be an idiot. It actually doesn't have anything to do with me. Your situation with your daughter is different because you're not an idiot. You may have hurt her, but in the end you're all right. My dad isn't all right. He's an idiot. Through and through."

Alfie kind of looked at me and smiled. "We'll, I'm not going to lecture you. Doesn't really have anything to do with me. But my guess is that I don't really need to tell you what to do. You'll forgive your dad one day. I just hope you do it sooner rather than later."

I didn't reply. Just kept eating my meat loaf.

31 I love parties. I don't like birthday parties. I especially don't like my own birthday parties. Never have. And when I was old enough to put an end to that kind of celebration without too much damage to my social standing, I did. Nothing's more important than a birthday party when you're young— doesn't matter if you hate them. But after I turned ten, they stopped.

However, as I mentioned, the party I was planning with Frank's mother happened to be about half a week after I turned sixteen. I had managed to keep this quiet. But Frank finally put the two things together and, knowing how much I hate my own birthday parties, he was more than happy to tell his mother.

I was hanging with Frank by his pool one afternoon after work, catching some late rays, which are excellent tanning rays, when Mrs. Ballard walked out with a plate of cookies and lemonade. When Frank saw her, he hoisted himself out of the pool and said, "Mom, did you know that Brett's birthday is next week? Just four days before the party."

I thought Mrs. Ballard was going to drop the food.

"No, I didn't!" she said. "Well, there will definitely have to be a cake."

"That's OK," I said. "I don't want you to go to any trouble."

"Trouble?" she said. "It's no trouble at all. I'd love to have a birthday cake. I live to have birthday cakes."

As she said this, Frank turned to me and flashed me a satisfied grin.

"I think we should tell people to bring presents, too," Frank said.

"No. No presents," I said. "That's really not necessary." Truthfully, the idea of presents sounded pretty good to me. On a purely material level, that is. But I had to stay focused. Had to win the heart of Nicole. Couldn't embarrass myself opening birthday presents while she was around. I'd look like a child. I wanted to look like a man. A man.

"Of course people will bring presents," Mrs. Ballard said.

I wanted to insist again that we not celebrate my birthday, but Frank knew exactly what he was doing. Mrs. Ballard had been so nice to me and she was so excited about throwing a party, that I realized to deny her the pleasure of celebrating my birthday was impossible. It would have been cruel and it would have hurt her feelings. "It's really not necessary," I said, one more time, meekly, closing my eyes.

"Don't be silly," she said again. "The matter is settled. I need to go think about a cake."

When she went back in the house Frank flashed me another grin. I wanted to tell him that he had betrayed the sacred trust of our friendship but before I could open my mouth he said, "That's what you get for crossing me, buddy. Now I'm kind of excited for our party."

"Great," I said, closing my eyes again.

32 I practiced driving with Alfie on Thursday and Friday, and had barely any near-death experiences. There were two, to be exact, which is five less than the number of near-death experiences I had when Alfie was behind the wheel.

The first came when I swerved to avoid a small family of squirrels who seemed to be picnicking in the middle of the street.

If I were to think logically, I would have run the picnic over. Not worth me killing myself, Alfie, and the minivan full of kids that I almost hit for a bunch of squirrels. But when you're cruising along, minding your own business, and suddenly you see a cluster of cute, furry animals, it's almost impossible not to swerve. Fortunately, I was able to swerve back on to my side of the road. But I was able to do this only because the minivan came to a screeching halt. The driver, a mom of some sort, was furious and started honking like she wanted to kill me.

"Stay focused," Alfie said. "Those were good swerves. Don't let her bully you."

The second near-death experience came when I backed into some guy's motorcycle. Just tapped it. A tiny tap. Not a scratch on the thing or on Alfie's van. But some guys are pretty touchy about their motorcycles. They don't like it when you tap them with your van. And the owner of this particular motorcycle was particularly touchy and also particularly large.

"You idiot," I heard when I gave the motorcycle that little tiny tap. Then I looked into my rearview mirror and saw this guy who was nine feet tall and had no shirt on and had huge bulging muscles run up to my door and bang on the window. I lowered it about half an inch.

"What do you think you're doing?" he yelled.

"What do you mean?" I said.

"You just ran into my bike."

"I did?"

"Yeah, you did."

"I don't think I did."

"Open the door."

I looked over at Alfie and he was giving me this look like, "You've got to open it. We all know you hit the motorcycle." So I opened the door and walked with the guy to check out the motorcycle. There were no scratches or dings. I got lucky.

"You're still an idiot," the guy said.

"No I'm not," I replied as I walked back to the van, although the truth is that I did feel a little stupid.

Anyway, I survived the week and ended up at Frank's house late Friday afternoon. Our plan was the same as always. Goof off, walk around, eat, talk about girls. I also did a bit more planning with Mrs. Ballard. We came up with a guest list and she said she'd handle sending out the invitations. We also talked a bit about the food. We were going to have the party catered, of course, because that's what rich people do. She knew a place that wheeled huge grills in and cooked barbequed everything. Sounded good to me.

"And, of course, there's the matter of the cake."

"Right," I said, a little disappointed that she didn't forget this small matter.

Mrs. Ballard told me that she was going to use this upscale bakery that could make a cake that would feed our humungous guest list.

"I talked to your mother last night on the phone," she said. "Apparently, you are a fan of chocolate."

"That's true," I said. It was true. I was a fan of chocolate cake. I just didn't want the chocolate cake to be my birthday cake. "I love chocolate cake," I continued.

Frank and I spent the rest of the night playing video games and walking around. We headed downtown hoping to bump into someone. But we didn't. No girls magically appeared to introduce themselves and tell us they loved us. No Nicole. Too bad.

33 So that weekend was restful. No visits to see Dad. That was restful. The week following it was also restful, if you can believe that a week of cleaning pools can be restful. I guess there were no disasters, which was why I was relaxed. Believe me, any day where you don't see your dad beaten up and lose all your money is a good day. Count your blessings.

At the end of the week, things got more tense as we prepared for another visit to Hartsville. I was going about every other week by that point. I pretty much followed my sister's lead, did what she did. And she insisted on once every two weeks. Made my mom happy that I went along, but I still tried to remain angry and bitter.

We stayed in the same crappy hotel, saw Dad in the same crappy visiting room, and ate the same crappy food. My dad complained like he usually did. I sat rolling my eyes and wondering if I could really ever survive another visit.

I didn't wise off too much. Only once. My dad wanted to know how my job was going. I said, "None of your damn business, Pop."

That wasn't very nice.

But I said it out of principle. See, I had been thinking about what Alfie said to me at lunch—about how I should get over myself and be nicer because people make mistakes and blah blah blah. I guess I started thinking about Alfie and what a great guy he was and how he deserved forgiveness for anything he might have done. I didn't care what he did. He deserved forgiveness because as bad as his mistakes might have been, he was a great guy. A solid, honest, kindhearted man. Maybe I should be nicer to Dad, I thought. Maybe I'll say something nice. That's when I piped up and said, "None of your damn business, Pop." Why did I say it? Because I didn't want to get soft. Can't get soft, cause that's when you get beaten. You become too complacent, you think things aren't so bad, you feel kindness and goodwill toward your fellow man, and bam, next thing you know your family is flat broke and your dad is in jail. That's what you get for letting your guard down. I was keeping my guard up. Not letting it down. Nope.

On the car ride home, my mom didn't say anything about my insubordination. This is the advantage of being mean all the time. When you're only a little mean, everyone is proud of how you behaved. My mom couldn't yell at me because, let's face it, I've said plenty worse than "none of your damn business."

We also spent some of the ride back from Hartsville talking about my birthday and my driver's license, which was way better than any other birthday present I could think of, especially because we were broke. If things hadn't changed, I would have been looking forward to a new car. But even the fact that I wasn't going to get any deluxe presents wasn't going to spoil the fun of getting my license.

My mom had even reserved a vacation day from work to take me to the division of motor vehicles. Wednesday. I had arranged the day off with Alfie as well. Mom and I were going together. This made her happy. It makes moms happy when you're looking forward to something that you're going to do together.

"You're getting too old," she kept saying. "It makes me sad. You're growing up too quickly."

She also said that we'd have a little party the evening I got my license, since it was my birthday and all. I think my mom was pretty happy that Mrs. Ballard was having a big party for me. Took some of the pressure off.

"I'll make a cake and cook whatever you want for dinner," she said. "For the family part of your birthday celebration." I was afraid my mother was going to come to the party at Frank's house, but I think she knew better. My mom loved chaperoning. It was one of her favorite things in the world. But I think Mrs. Ballard told her that I was trying to get Nicole to fall in love with me and realized I didn't need my mother around for that. The only thing she said in regard to Nicole was the following cryptic statement: "Let me know if you're going on any dates and I'll let you take the car, assuming you pass the test."

Thanks, I thought. I'm sure our economy car will make the ladies drool. Drool. Even Alfie's pool-cleaning van would have given me a better shot with Nicole.

34 You'd think that once my dad was in jail, the damage he could do was pretty much curtailed. This, however, was not true.

I was due to take my driving test on Wednesday. Tuesday night the prison called to tell my mom that Dad was in the infirmary. Why? Appendicitis. He was set to be operated on in the morning. Mom could come and be with him in the hospital. Wednesday. The day I was supposed to get my license.

"You're not really going, are you?" I said when I heard the news.

"Brett, I have to. I'm so sorry about this. But you can wait a few more days. Your dad's going to have an operation."

"It's his appendix. Every guy and their uncle has their appendix out. It's not even like a real operation."

"Brett, try to understand this. If it were anything else, I wouldn't back out of our plans. But this is kind of serious."

"Why does Dad have to ruin everything? He ruins absolutely everything. I don't think I'm asking for too much to get my license on my birthday. Isn't every sixteen-year-old entitled to that?"

My mom gave me one of her looks of desperation. I know. She's got it rough too. Still, of all the things to happen. Once again, my dad jumps in at the last minute to ruin everything. It was getting to be the story of my life.

Anyway, when I called Alfie Tuesday evening to tell him I could, in fact, work the next day, he said that if I wanted to, we could go get my license together and I could use his van to take the test. Frankly, it sounded like a crazy idea to me.

"Can you do that?" I asked. "Take a driving test in a pool-cleaning van?"

"I don't see why not," he replied.

"What about the schedule?"

"I'll shift it around. We can start early, skip lunch, and finish off the day after you take your test."

I thought about it for a few minutes, but couldn't really come up with an argument against the idea—other than the fact that it seemed insane. "OK," I said. "It's a deal. Thanks."

I told my mom the plan. She seemed relieved and started raving about what a great guy Alfie was. I found this sort of annoying.

"Listen," I said. "This doesn't let anyone off the hook. Dad still blew it with this stupid appendix thing. Don't think I'll forgive him for it."

My mom frowned. "You're wearing me out, Brett," she said.

"You're just getting old, Mom," I replied. My mom looked

mad but then smiled a little and tried to put me in a headlock. But I squirmed away. Can't put a guy like me in a headlock. No way.

35 So Wednesday morning I was at Alfie's house at the crack of dawn. He grilled me all morning about various aspects of driving. I had heard the California written test was a joke, but I didn't know the answers to half of Alfie's questions.

"Did you read the driver's manual?" Alfie asked impatiently.

"Of course I did." It was true. I did. But obviously I didn't read it carefully enough. As for my actual driving, it was great. I was a real pro behind the wheel of the pool van. No examiner in his right mind could fail me.

We whipped through the morning pools and at about twelve-thirty we headed to the DMV for my test. Alfie had packed us a few sandwiches to eat as we drove. Some kind of bean-sprout sandwiches. It sounds disgusting, but they tasted pretty good. Still, I'll never eat them again. Sure, the taste was fine, but who wants to eat bean sprouts?

The written test came first, and as I checked off boxes I wished I had studied a little more. They ask you some pretty stupid stuff on these tests. Not stuff you'd ever have any reason to know. But I passed. Which was good news, and also a joke, because I didn't know anything. Maybe they felt sorry for me— the poor boy forced to take his driving test in a pool-cleaning van.

When the examiner and I arrived at the van, he kind of gave me a funny look. "You're taking the test in this?" he said.

"You don't like it?" I replied.

"It just seems like it might be hard to drive."

"Not for a guy like me. See, I happen to be a fantastic driver."

The examiner looked at me and then said, "OK, hotshot, let's get going." We climbed in, and off we went.

I drove slowly, kept my eyes on the road, obeyed traffic signs, and generally put forward a superior performance. The man told me to make lefts, rights, come to full stops, and when we made it back to the DMV he made me parallel park between two orange cones. Needless to say, I passed that section with flying colors— there were no muscle-bound bikers to make me nervous.

When it was all over, the examiner reprimanded me for not slowing down in a school zone. But he said that was my only mistake. "So you pass," he said. "Congratulations."

The examiner and I walked back into the DMV office building and found Alfie pacing and wringing his hands. Kind of touching, really. He looked like an expectant father.

"You waiting for him?" the examiner said as we approached Alfie.

"Yep. How'd he do?"

"He passed. Just need to take a picture and he's legal."

Alfie looked at me and smiled. "Congratulations!" he said.

"Thanks," I replied, smiling, kind of feeling all happy that someone else was all happy for me. Then the examiner and I went to the photographer's area and took a terrible picture of me. They filled out some more paperwork, checked my birth certificate, and sent me on my way.

As I expected, it was a pretty exciting moment for me. But as Alfie and I walked back through the parking lot to the van, I couldn't help but also feel a little disappointment. Now the fact that I wasn't getting a brand spanking new car made me feel bad. Again, I know that not every kid in the world gets a new car the day they get their license. But I always thought I would. On top of that, I didn't even get to use my mother's car, seeing that she was in Hartsville visiting my dad.

Anyway, Alfie and I had a pool to get to before the day was done, so there was no time to start complaining. And Alfie was very proud of me. Kept saying, "I'm very proud of you."

I said that I was proud of myself and congratulated myself on being so smart and such a hard worker. "It's not a matter of luck," I told Alfie. "It's a matter of hard work and perseverance. I am one hard worker."

Alfie smiled. "Yes you are. One cocksure, overconfident, hard worker."

"Yup."

36 After we finished the last pool of the day, Alfie drove me to our side of the tracks. But he didn't drop me off. Instead he drove to his house.

As he pulled into his driveway he said, "Come inside. I got you a birthday present. And after that, if you like, you can keep the van for the night. I'm sure you probably want to go out and drive your friends around."

At first I thought that there was no way I wanted to go cruising in the pool van. But then I reconsidered and thought it might be fun after all.

My present was sitting on a small table right inside the doorway. "Open it," Alfie said, pointing to it.

I picked it up, shook it a few times, and then opened it up. It was a leather jacket—an old one, but really cool. Vintage, cracked leather, with a few patches on the sides, including a patch that said U.S. Air Force.

"It's incredible," I said. And that's really what I thought. It was incredible. I put it on. It was a little too big for me. But it still looked great.

"I thought it was a good gift for a young driver. Everyone needs a good driving jacket."

"Where did you get it?" I asked.

"It's mine. I've had it for years. I used to fly airplanes. Years ago."

"You used to fly airplanes?" I said.

"Years ago. I was in the air force for a while. Then I flew small commercial planes for a few years. Gave it up because I wanted to drift for a while. I wanted do something else."

"Like clean pools?" I said, but then regretted this instantly because it seemed like such a snotty thing to say. But Alfie just smiled.

"I wanted to goof off and not do anything," he said. "I did all sorts of different jobs."

I was still looking at him incredulously.

"What?" he said. "Do you think I've been cleaning pools my whole life?"

"I guess I kind of did," I said.

"I suppose I've been doing it for a while. Why? You don't like cleaning pools? I love it. Easy job, nice way to live in California, leaves me plenty of time to tend to my garden. Anyway, I'm in my seventies. It's a great retirement job—can't do anything too stressful."

"I guess," I said.

"Anyway, why don't you get going because I need to take a nap. I'm exhausted."

I looked at Alfie and was suddenly gripped with feelings of happiness and gratitude—not my normal state of mind in those days.

"Thanks, Alfie," I said. He put out his hand, we shook like gentlemen, and I turned and walked out the door to the van. Driver's license, wheels, and a cool leather jacket. What more could a man like me want?

37 I had made plans with Frank to hang out that night. I didn't exactly expect to be driving around in Alfie's van. After I found out my dad had to have his appendix out, I kind of figured I'd be swimming in Frank's pool before eating some fabulous dinner that Mrs. Ballard made for me. Now I was excited to go out on the town—after swimming and eating Mrs. Ballard's fabulous dinner, of course.

When I showed up at Frank's, Mrs. Ballard was out on her front lawn digging near some shrubs. Occasionally rich people do that. Pretend they garden. Frank's family had a fleet of yard workers. Like eight hundred of them. Still, Mrs. Ballard liked to chip in every so often. Helped her get back to the land.

As I pulled up, Mrs. Ballard looked over to me and waved.

"I expected to see Alfie," she said as I got out of the van. "Guess you passed your test."

"Yep. It's official now."

"Well, congratulations. And happy birthday. Excited for Saturday?"

"Very."

"Frank just got back from tennis. He's out back in the pool."

"Thanks. I'll go find him."

I walked around back and saw Frank swimming around in his tennis shorts.

"What's up?" he said as he bobbed to the top of the water.

"Got my license."

"All right!" he exclaimed. "I'll ask my mom if we can take her car out tonight."

"That's OK. I have Alfie's van."

Frank didn't quite know what to make of this. Finally he said, "For what?"

"To drive around."

Frank started laughing. "You can't be serious. I'm sure my mom will let us take her car."

Suddenly I became very defensive about Alfie's van. "What's wrong with the van?"

"Nothing's wrong with it. It's a great pool-cleaning van. But I'm not cruising around in that thing."

"Well, I'm cruising around in it, and if you want to cruise with me, you'd better stop making fun of it."

Frank looked confused again, but rather than saying anything, he took a deep breath and dove to the bottom of the pool.

Dinner that night was the usual Ballard fare. Steaks, asparagus, baked potatoes, apple pie. It was something out of a television commercial. Mr. Ballard said he was sorry to hear my dad was sick. I said I was too. Had to be nice to Mr. Ballard. Hard to be a wiseass to grown men, especially if they're nice.

We also went over last-minute party preparations. The invites had been sent out two weeks ago. Most had replied and said that they were coming.

"Nicole called last night and said she'd be here," Mrs. Ballard said.

"Yeah, but I think she's only coming because she likes me," Frank said.

"That'll be the day," I replied.

"What, she could like me."

"Keep telling yourself that."

"I'll tell you what. Since you like her, I'll keep away. I just want you to know that it would make more sense if she liked me."

I smiled, because the very idea was pure comedy.

When we finished dinner, Frank and I headed out for a night on the town. What this would include, I didn't exactly know for sure. I had been paid the previous week, and since I hadn't been buying any expensive bathing suits, I had saved some cash. I secretly wished that Frank and I might be invited to some crazy party, but fat chance of that happening on a Wednesday night, or any night for that matter. Most likely we'd drive around town hoping to bump into someone we knew.

As Frank and I climbed in the van, Mrs. Ballard decided she needed to get a picture of me behind the wheel. She was laughing and making me pose, and I even put on my leather jacket for the occasion.

When the pictures were over and I was pulling out of the driveway, I looked up at Mrs. Ballard waving and suddenly felt kind of sad again. And kind of guilty. It was like the party preparations. My mom used to love that stuff. Then suddenly she didn't have enough time. I wondered if my mom felt bad that she couldn't be there to see me drive alone for the first time. I knew my dad probably felt bad. But he was in jail and he was an idiot. He'd probably enjoy mowing the lawn just to get out of the slammer. But I felt bad that my mom wasn't there.

This sadness didn't really leave me. Not for the next few hours. As Frank and I drove in circles blasting Alfie's crappy AM radio while we discussed my plans to win Nicole's heart, I couldn't help thinking about my mom. After driving down the main street of Glenwood for like the thirtieth time (meeting no ladies, by the way), I finally told Frank that I was tired and needed to drop him off.

"You're like an old man," he said. "Where's your sense of fun?"

I was plenty fun. But I was sad. And I was tired.

"I've got to head home," I told Frank again. "I'm exhausted."

When I got home that night after dropping Frank off, I decided to call my mom's room at the hotel. When she answered I thought she was going to choke, she was so surprised.

"What's wrong," she said. "Why are you calling?"

"I just wanted to tell you that I got my license."

My mom paused as if she was waiting for her heart to calm down.

"That's wonderful, Brett. I'll be home tomorrow night and you can have the car then. If you drive me to work, I'll even let you have the car for the weekend."

"I'll drive you anywhere you want to go," I said, then I paused. "How's Dad?

"Dad's just fine. It was a pretty easy operation. Nothing dangerous. He's just a bit groggy. Should I tell him you say hello?"

I paused again. "No," I said. "I just called to talk to you."

"OK," she said. We talked for a few more minutes and then said good-bye, and as I hung up the phone the guilt came rushing back. I could have let her say hi to him for me. But just as quickly I decided that I wasn't going to feel any pity for good old Dad.

38 Thursday afternoon, I got home from cleaning pools to find my mother at home. She was busy in the kitchen, making my birthday cake. Family night. Family birthday party. I could live with that.

Hannah and my Aunt Mary were wandering around decorating the house. The entire downstairs was being remodeled in honor of me.

"Forget it, you people," I yelled when I came through the door. "You're all a day late." But I kind of smiled when I said this.

"But we love you," Hannah said, giggling.

"We love you," my aunt repeated.

This I actually did find alarming. "OK, OK. You can celebrate my birthday, but knock off the love talk."

"We love you, Brett," my mother called from the kitchen. "Do you love us?"

"Whatever. I guess." With that, I ran upstairs to take a shower and relax before the festivities began. You wouldn't think pool cleaning was a dirty job. But I sure smelled bad when I got done. All the sweating, I guess.

I went downstairs about an hour later, all dressed up, combed, and clean. I decided to wear a tie. Seemed appropriate. My birthday. Funny, but I used to wear a tie all the time—country club parties, fancy dinners, encounters with my father's rich friends. But I hadn't worn a tie in months. No reason to.

My aunt came up and gave me a hug. She was wearing new slippers, which was her way of honoring me. Hannah put on a dress that was pretty much the last article of clothing she bought when we were rich. She looked great, so I told her she did.

"You look great," I said.

"Oh, Brett," she said sarcastically. "You're so sweet."

Dinner was pretty much the kind of thing my mother would have made if she was giving a dinner party. She made all sorts of stuff she hadn't made in a long time. Shrimp cocktail, lamb, roast potatoes, etc. Funny how good it all smelled and how good it all tasted once we sat down at the dining room table. I never would have thought twice about eating that kind of food when I was rich. Now that we were broke, it tasted much better. Don't get me wrong. Being broke has taught me no important lessons, so I'm not saying that losing all my money taught me to appreciate the world. I appreciated the world much more when I was loaded. But that dinner tasted pretty good. Can't deny it.

Afterwards I opened presents. It's one thing to make a nice dinner. The food is a little more expensive than normal, and a tired mom likes to cook much less than a rich, well-rested mom. But you can still do it on a budget once in a while. Good presents cost money. Now don't get me wrong. I'm not complaining about the presents because my mom and my sister and my aunt didn't have much money. I had to take what I could get. And the presents were nice: shirts, shoes, a belt, a few CDs, etc. Not bad. But it sure wasn't a brand-new car. Still, I laid off the sarcasm. I knew my mother would have wanted to give me more. Just no way she could, that's all.

39

Historically, my interaction with women has been disastrous. Surprising, given my looks and personality. But true. And when I was rich, it was even more surprising. Babes dig rich dudes. It's well documented. Still, despite the fact that I was a pauper, I had my looks and charm, and now that I could drive, I was a bona fide man. No way Nicole wouldn't like me.

Several hours before the party began, on that Saturday afternoon, Frank decided to get me psyched up about asking Nicole out. But I insisted I had my own plan.

"I have it all worked out," I said. "I'm just going to lean over and kiss her."

"When?"

"When the mood strikes me, that's when."

"Yeah, that'll work. Kiss her when the mood strikes you. That's a plan."

"Well, why ask her out? It just postpones the inevitable making out. I think I'm going to skip right to that step."

"First, it's a bad plan. Second, you'll never do it. You're too much of a coward."

"Listen Frank, once you get your license, a whole world of manhood opens up to you. I'll kiss her. No problem."

Anyway, I spent that afternoon hoping and praying that

things would go well with Nicole and me. Basically, I was hoping for a miracle. Or, I was hoping that I was capable of miraculous action.

When the party finally started—evening, about seven o'clock—I went out back to play it cool. It was exactly as promised. A well-catered affair complete with grills, chefs, hired waiters, and like a million high school kids there to luxuriate at the Ballard estate.

I ate precisely six pieces of chicken in the first ten minutes of the party. I stood by the grill and ate the chicken as it came off the assembly line. A couple of my friends caught on to this—pretty much the same gang from the Fourth. I thought that maybe since I was trying to look cool, it might not be such a great idea to stand there stuffing my face. But I couldn't help myself.

At that point, however, not everyone had shown up, the most important part of that everyone being Nicole. So who cared if I looked like a starving idiot? That's what I was.

A buddy of mine named Billy Stillman was DJing the party. Frank's parents had a really great sound system rigged up around the pool. Rich people have music piped in everywhere. We used to. Anyway, Billy was blasting music, Mrs. Ballard lit cheesy tiki lamps everywhere, and people were strutting around in their swimsuits. It was like a movie.

And then, finally, Nicole showed up.

Now, Nicole was a friend of mine, and I had no problems talking to her. She must have known I liked her, because everyone did. She brought me a present, which most of the other guests neglected to do. I was definitely happy about that. I figured it was a signal. I didn't open it right away. Mrs. Ballard established a present table in the living room. Later. I would open them later.

Anyway, to get to the point, this party was just like any other great party, and I was on a great mission. A mission of heroic proportions. I had psyched myself up. I wasn't going to back down. I chatted with Nicole. I brought her a chicken wing and some shrimp. As an offering. She told me that we were going to have a great year at school. I told her my summer was going well. She told me hers was going well too. More people filtered in, and Nicole and I split up and came back together as we greeted the new arrivals and got sidetracked by other discussions. It was all part of my plan. It was the attention/no-attention plan, where you act like a girl is the most important thing in the world and then you ignore her and play hard to get. A surefire method to convince a woman to love you.

The important thing was not to back down when the moment presented itself to kiss her. And once it was dark and people started relaxing and everyone had arrived, I decided it was time to make my move.

Nicole was at the other side of the pool. There were a few people standing around her. I was going to walk to the cabana–changing-room building located at another side of the pool, where it was a little more deserted, and when the time was right, I was going to call her over, chat with her for a few minutes, and then plant one on her, finally consummating the love that I knew we shared.

Once I took my position, I waited. I needed a break in the chattering that was going on around her. I needed someone to leave the conversation and in that break I was going to yell, "Hey, Nicole, come over here for a second, will you." She was going to come over and we would probably be married in a matter of months.

But the crowd around Nicole just kind of got bigger. Other people showed up and they were all standing where she was standing and there wasn't a break. At first. Finally, the clump of kids started to thin out, and there was a noticeable break in the talk, and it was my time to step in. But just as I was getting up the guts to put my hand to my mouth to call out to Nicole, she turned and started kissing this guy—a senior lacrosse player, of all things—and not just a little peck-on-the-cheek kiss but a real boyfriend-girlfriend kiss.

Needless to say, I did not call Nicole over.

Now, it is impossible to quite describe the magnitude of my

disappointment. And my anger. As far as I was concerned, Nicole and I were destined to be together, so this lacrosse player was not just horning in on my woman, but was interfering with the cosmic order of things.

My mind searched for a plan. I thought about tackling him and telling him to go away. But that tactic didn't seem like it would work. Still, it was the only thing I could think of. I have to tackle him, I kept thinking as Nicole kept kissing him. I have to tackle him. But just as I was trying to psych myself up about tackling him, Frank appeared.

"Whatever you're thinking, it won't work," he said.

I looked at him and suddenly became furious. Just what I needed. Wiseass Frank was there to make fun of me in my moment of despair. He just looked at me and finally said, "I'm really sorry. I just found out a few minutes ago. I'm really sorry."

How about that. Frank was being kind. And I appreciated it. Because the fact is, I was pretty upset.

Anyway. So. The rest of the party. It sucked and there's nothing to describe. Everyone sang "Happy Birthday" when Mrs. Ballard brought out the cake. Everyone said what a great guy I was. Nicole gave me a great big hug as though she hadn't just stomped all over my heart. And then everyone went home. That's it. Nothing more to tell. Nothing at all.

40 So I had had it. I was only sixteen and my life was already a long string of disasters. Needless to say, that Sunday sucked, as did the rest of the week and the week after that. Cleaning pools sucks when you're pissed off and heartbroken. Any work sucks when you're feeling that way.

Still, one thing I've learned is that the best way to get over one disappointment or hardship is to find a bigger hardship. This is something I've learned. The only way to get over one disaster is to find another.

The only thing is that I shouldn't be flip about this next one.

It's not funny. And I know I'm a wiseass, but for a moment let me be perfectly serious: this was the worst thing ever to happen in my short miserable life. And I doubt I'm going to come up with anything worse any time soon. I'm not exaggerating this time.

41 Let me tell you about the way things happen.
When you're telling a story to a friend, things seem to

happen with a purpose and an order. There's an ending to your story. You know this. The person listening to you knows this. That is, he doesn't know the actual ending, but he knows that there is an ending. Unless, of course, he thinks you're a complete idiot.

But in life, things don't happen like that. They happen in a state of confusion. And they happen all at once. And they happen without you having too much say in the matter.

It's just like with my dad. One day I casually open the door and there are cops and guys in suits standing there. The next thing I know, my dad is facedown in the kitchen, bleeding on the floor, while my mother and sister are crying. And the next thing I know after that, we're flat broke and living with my aunt. That's how things happen. Not like in a story. There's no buildup. There's no development. One day you're doing one thing. The next day you're doing something else.

So it was a day in mid-August. It was a Tuesday. And I went to Alfie's house like I always did. At seven. But when I arrived, there was no answer at the door. There was no Alfie sitting on the stoop drinking his coffee.

After knocking for a little while, I went around back. Maybe he was in his garden, I thought. But again, no Alfie. Then I decided to knock on the back door, and just as I got to the top of the steps and looked in the window, I saw Alfie lying on the kitchen floor. He was lying there, kind of motionless, but also kind of moving.

The door was locked. But I didn't look for the key. In about ten seconds, I put a brick through the window and I was opening the door from the inside.

Alfie looked up at me and whispered, "I can't move. It's my heart."

I had watched TV every day of my life and I knew just what to do. In another five seconds I was on the phone and dialing 911. And in ten minutes, I was in the back of an ambulance, watching Alfie as he drifted in and out of consciousness, blinking his eyes, moaning, as two EMT dudes jammed a million needles in him and strapped an oxygen mask on his face and radioed into the hospital that they had an 8-91, which I assumed was code for "we have a guy who's really messed up and you better be ready because we're bringing him in now."

So that's how things happen. And what happens *after* things like that happen? You spend a lot of time wondering what's going on.

Like, hours.

The only thing I knew for sure was that Alfie had had a heart attack, and that it wasn't the mild kind of heart attack. They asked me if he had any family. I said that he had a daughter in Portland, Oregon. What was her name? "Linda Moore is her name," I told them. "Or it's her maiden name, at least. But she's divorced."

They said they'd call her. I guess hospitals have the phone numbers of everyone in the world. Good idea, huh?

"Any news?" I kept saying to anyone who would listen to me. Nurses, patients, janitors. Mostly they just flashed me strange looks. Other times they said they'd find the doctor. And if it was the doctor and I said, "Any news, Doc?" he'd just say, "We're running some tests. You can't see him yet."

That's all I heard. Over and over.

I called my mom to let her know what was up, that I probably wouldn't be home for a while. She was in tears when she heard. Funny. She didn't even know Alfie all that well. How come mothers can cry like that? Any sad thing, whether it has to do with them or not, they start to blubber.

She asked if I needed anything. I told her that I was fine. Sandwiches? I couldn't even stand the idea of food, so I didn't need her to bring me sandwiches. I was fine. I'd call her when I knew more. But I stayed there all day without knowing anything.

Finally, at about six in the evening, I saw Linda, Alfie's daughter, walking quickly down the hall to the waiting room. I had only seen her in pictures, but I recognized her right away.

Short dark hair, kind of skinny. She was a little older than I expected. Funny to see one old person be the child of another old person. But she wasn't really that old. Maybe in her fifties. But old to me. Anyone who's over thirty is in the same boat, as far as I'm concerned.

I stood up to say something, but I kind of choked and she sped right by me. I guess there's no reason she'd recognize me or know who I was. I tried to say something again, but I just kind of choked again. What could I say? I just watched as she went to the nurse's desk. They talked briefly and then, before I knew what was going on, the nurse stood up and told Linda to follow her, and they disappeared between two swinging doors. I decided to follow too, but then stopped. Maybe I'd talk to her when she came back. Let the doctor explain things to her.

Then I thought that he might be telling her something I didn't know. So I decided that I *would* follow. But when I pushed open the swinging doors, they were gone.

It was about an hour before Linda returned. Her eyes were wet with tears and it looked like she was still crying. At this point I decided to introduce myself. Maybe Linda found something out.

"Linda Moore?" I said.

She looked up, completely startled. "Yes?" she said.

"Hi. I'm Brett Gerson. You don't know . . .

"I've heard all about you," she said, trying to smile and wiping her eyes. "Have you been here all day?"

"Yes."

"I heard you were the one who found my father."

"Yes. I did. Had to break a window, even. How's he doing?"

"Not so good," she said, now trying to hold back tears again. "He was talking. But it was a pretty bad heart attack. If he makes it through the next day, things will look better. Now we have to wait."

As she said the words "if he makes it," I felt a huge lump in my throat. I wanted to see him. Linda seemed to have understood what I was thinking.

"He's sleeping now. You can see him later. He needs rest. He was sleeping when I left."

"I haven't seen him at all today," I said. "Not since this morning." My voice was pretty scratchy because now I was starting to fight tears.

Linda stepped closer and hugged me. "I'm sorry," she said. "They should have let you see him." Then she started crying. Real crying, not just a few tears. And that made me cry, because having someone hug you while they're crying is about as sad a thing as there is, especially if it's because someone they love is sick.

42 So let me tell you something else about the way things happen. When things get strange and confused and happen in a blur, the main thing you're looking for is a way out, a resting point, a place to regroup. When my dad got busted, we got a lawyer, talked to a judge we knew, looked through our finances, that kind of thing. But when things are really crazy, there's no resting point. There's no place to stop and regroup. Things start getting stranger. And that leads to a weird sort of disappointment. You spend the whole day thinking about how crazy things are as though the crazy thing is about to end. But if it's really crazy, it keeps on coming. My experience says it gets worse.

No way I was leaving the hospital that night. No way. Doctors told me and Linda to head home and get some rest. But Linda wasn't leaving, and neither was I. We were there for the long haul. We were going to be there in the morning to see Alfie. We stole a couple of pillows from a hospital linen closet, set up a little camp in a corner of the waiting room, and started talking.

And it was the best kind of talking. We were both worried. Really worried. And we started getting all teary eyed as we talked about Alfie. Linda told me all sorts of wild stories about Alfie when he was young. He had her when he was just twenty-three years old, so she knew him when he was pretty young.

"He was still a young man," she said. "And he never never got tired of playing with me. When he was around. He left when I was pretty young. But he came back every so often. We used to camp on the beach and spend whole weeks doing nothing but swimming and hanging out."

She also told me about all the crazy jobs Alfie had. He was a cook on a cruise ship, a lumberjack, a dealer in a casino, a ski instructor, and even a barber, which I couldn't believe.

"A barber?" I said.

"A barber," she replied.

I couldn't believe it at all. "When . . . and where?"

And as I asked this Linda's eyes lit up and she said, "Well, the story gets crazier. You're really not going to believe how he got that job." But just as she said this, another doctor stepped out and called Linda's name, and when we went up to him he was looking at us in a way that made us not want to come any closer.

"Mrs. Moore," he said. "I have some bad news. Your father has died."

Huh? I didn't understand. Where were all the running doctors and flashing lights and beeping monitors? Where was the screaming? Where was the mayhem? Don't they alert you? Why weren't we told that he was about to die? Did they try to bring him back to life? We had stolen pillows from the linen closet. We had made a little camp. We were going to stay there all night. We were there for Alfie. We were there, all the way.

And then nothing. Boom. All there is is a doctor with bad news.

Funny. When you get news like that, you don't cry. You just stand there thinking. You're thinking of a way to make what just happened go away. You're looking for a way out. You're looking for a solution. We're human beings after all. We're problem solvers. And we're in a hospital. We're surrounded by medical problem solvers. But all we could do was just stand there. Shaking. Thinking about how to make the thing we just heard untrue.

And when your mind has exhausted all the possibilities, when it has hit brick walls in every direction it's turned, that's when you start crying. It's really fast. It seems like a lifetime of thinking. But it's actually really fast. And suddenly you're hugging each other and crying and asking the doctor insane questions that all have bad answers that you don't even want to know.

And then you don't believe it. It's not that you've thought the problem away. You just don't believe it. You have to see it for yourself. Both Linda and I had to see Alfie. But here's a bad rule that some dumb-ass adult came up with. You can't see it all for yourself unless the deceased is family. Even Linda put up a stink, a big fat screaming, crying stink where she said I was one of

Alfie's best friends in the world. But forget it. The dumb-ass adult rule-makers won this one long ago.

"There are no exceptions. It's the law. I'm very sorry. I'm very sorry," the doctor kept saying. He sounded like my dad. Adults sure spend a lot of time saying they're sorry for some dumb-ass stuff.

But then Linda had this look in her eye like she really needed to see her father. And I'm standing there thinking, the more we fight with this idiot doctor, the longer that's going to be delayed.

"Go ahead," I said. "Go ahead. It's OK."

43 There are those who think that humans should face up to the natural cycles of life and death. They think that humans shouldn't ignore the unpleasant facts of the world. They think people should learn to accept things like dying. Well, let me take this opportunity to say that these freaks are all completely wrong. Take it from me: if you're smart, you'll live your life in complete ignorance of death. You'll never face any of the facts about where we're all headed. That kind of truth will ruin your life. And not just "poor me, I'm not rich" ruined. I mean really ruined. Ruined and sad. Like sad that a guy who you really care about and who really cares about you suddenly disappears.

Alfie's funeral was scheduled for three days after he died. The days between his death and the funeral are still pretty much a blur to me. I spent a lot of time with Linda. She handled most of the funeral arrangements, but I was with her for a bunch of the decision making.

You have to do all sorts of things you don't want to do when you're getting ready to bury someone. You have to pick out a casket. You have to find a burial plot. You have to get a headstone. We even had to find an outfit for Alfie to wear. I suggested a Hawaiian shirt, Bermuda shorts, and tennis shoes. A pool man's outfit. Linda thought it was a good idea, but we decided against it. Best to keep these things simple.

The other thing you have to do is see the body. Or, you don't have to. But you have the opportunity to, if you want. I did want to. I asked to see Alfie. The funeral director brought me into the visitation room.

"Here's your friend," he said, in a quiet, sympathetic whisper.

There is absolutely no point in trying to describe what that was like, seeing Alfie's body. I could never get it right. I barely even remember the details. Mostly what I have is what's left of a feeling, a feeling like this was the worst thing that I could ever possibly imagine.

I do remember one thing, however. I remember that when I stood with Alfie in the visitation room, it was like I was with a perfect stranger. When he was alive, Alfie was never without some kind of grin or smirk, or a look of amusement like he was about to tell you some kind of crazy story. When Alfie was in his coffin, he was totally expressionless. Totally without expression. That's what I remember.

And I remember what I said.

"Forget it," I said. "I don't know this guy." And then I turned away.

The funeral director kind of gave me a look like I had said something incredibly insensitive. But it was true. That wasn't Alfie in the coffin. I didn't know who it was.

Anyway, I'd say about fifty people showed up at the funeral. Most I didn't know, but they all introduced themselves. Some were from California. Some were from places as far away as Alaska and London. They all had some story or other to tell about Alfie. It was kind of like they were enjoying getting together and reminiscing. "Good old Alfie," they said. "He was a real character." I guess that's what happens when you hit your seventies. Everyone you know starts to die, so you get used to it, and funerals are little trips down memory lane. Well I wasn't used to it. I was sixteen. I wasn't supposed to have any dead friends.

My mother and aunt and sister came as well. They cried through the whole thing. I know I make fun of my mother for crying all the time. And it's not like my sister or my aunt aren't the same way. All the same, I understood why they were crying. It's not like you need to know a guy to know that it's sad when he dies.

There was a strange semireligious minister guy who gave a speech and said a sort of prayer. He must have been in his seventies himself, and he didn't wear any kind of uniform. He didn't even wear a tie. Just a cotton shirt and pants.

After he said his prayer, he invited anyone who wanted to to stand up and say what was on their mind. Alfie's daughter got up and said something. She said what a wonderful dad Alfie was and that she was happy that she got to tell him so before he died. Then she told a story about how when she was fifteen he blew in from nowhere, gave her a new pickup truck, and then left. She said that she grew up loving and hating him for that kind of stuff. She loved him because he taught her so much and she hated him because she always wanted to know more. But at the end, she said, all she felt was love. Love. That's all.

Then a bunch of other people stood up to tell stories about

how they flew in planes with Alfie and dug wells with him and mined silver with him and raised goats with him. It was like a freak show. But a good one. One where you love the freaks and wish they were all your friends, wish you could all go clean pools together.

Then I gave a speech, because his daughter asked me to and I said I would. You do whatever someone asks when their father dies. Can't say no.

I talked about how Alfie was the craziest guy I ever knew and how he drank nine cups of coffee every morning and how he was a terrible driver and how he always made me scoop the dead things out of the pool. I talked about how he never combed his hair and how he always told me to be forgiving and how he had like eighteen billion jars of pickled vegetables in his house. "Eighteen billion," I said, "and that's not a joke." And I talked about all the other things that I loved about Alfie, except by the time I got to the ninth or tenth thing on the list I was crying and had to choke out the rest. Funny. No one could have heard half of my speech. And the half they heard, they couldn't have understood. It only meant something to me. Or at least that's what I thought. But there were all these people chuckling and crying as I talked and afterwards everyone said that I gave the most beautiful speech that they'd ever heard. Ever.

So the next thing I know, Alfie's coffin is being carried out of the funeral home and we're suddenly in a long line of cars, headed to the cemetery.

Let me be explicit about this: they lowered him into the ground and he's still there. In the cemetery. I always knew that cemeteries were full of dead people. But I didn't really know it. Not really. But when you see a guy who drove you to school, and cleaned your pool, and bossed you around dropped into the ground, then you know it. You realize that you never knew anything and that you suddenly know it all. A little prayer, then right in the ground. That's it. Then you know what's really in cemeteries. Then you know what a dead person really is.

This is something else I learned: after funerals, people go to someone's house for sandwiches. We volunteered our house to make life easy on Linda. To make life easy on me, I wasn't asked to do anything. Not one thing. I didn't even have to take out the garbage. My aunt and my sister and my mother sat up all night the night before the funeral making sandwiches and cookies and punch. Funny that anyone bothers to eat at all, given where we're all headed. There's nothing dopier than a cheese sandwich when you're thinking about death. Cheese. Just think about it. Think about it and then think about being lowered into the ground when you're seventy-five because your heart has had it. I'll never look at cheese sandwiches the same way again. Nope.

And then everybody leaves. And when they leave it's not like getting out of school for the day and saying bye and that you'll see them tomorrow. I met these people one time and won't meet them again, as far as I can tell. And then you're sad all over again. Or you're more sad, because you never really stop being sad in the first place. You realize that these people are the only people who really know the guy that you know, and then they're gone. Sure, there were a few Californians there, but they were mostly clients, people who knew Alfie as the pool guy. But what could I say to them? Most of his friends drifted back to Alaska and England. Good-bye. That was it. It was me, Mom, Hannah, and Aunt Mary. I headed to my closet. I needed to be alone.

44

OK. Need to make one correction. Not everyone left after the funeral. Linda stuck around. When someone dies, there's actually a lot of business to be done. Alfie had a lot of things, and Linda needed to deal with that. She also had papers and documents to sign. This is what she told me at the funeral. And when she called me the next day, she said it again, and then asked if I'd help her out, help her to sort through Alfie's stuff.

She said there were also specific things she needed to discuss with me—some of Alfie's last wishes.

I headed over to Alfie's that afternoon. It was pretty weird to be back at his place. The window in the kitchen was still broken—that was weird. Strange that that was the last time that I ever spoke to Alfie.

Linda had all sorts of documents spread across the kitchen table. The table in the dining room, where we sat, was the same way.

"I'm putting the house on the market," she said. "I want to get this done as quickly as possible. It's pretty painful."

"I'm sure," I said, and thought that there was no way I'd be able to sort through all of Alfie's stuff. Just being in his house made me want to start bawling.

"If there's something you want of my father's—to remind you of him—I want you to take it. I'm going to sell everything anyway, so you should take what you want. Or if you need something. I'd be happy for you to have anything you might need."

"Thanks," I said, although I strangely had no desire to take anything. "Maybe I'll just grab a few jars of pickled vegetables. He gave me a great birthday present—a leather jacket from when he was in the air force. That'll be enough to remind me of him."

"I know that jacket," she said, suddenly smiling. Then the smile faded and she paused and then looked back at Alfie's papers. "Well, the estate sale won't be for a few days yet, so you can think about it."

Then Linda paused again as she rifled through a stack of papers. "And there's one more thing," she said. "It has to do with something my father said when he was in the hospital. The night he died." As Linda said this, she kind of choked on the words. But after a few moments, she continued. "My father wanted to make sure he left you a few things, if he died. He thought you might like to take over his business, so he wanted you to have his pool van and his tech bag."

As Linda said this, she kind of laughed a little. "That was pretty important to him. That you have the pool van and the tech bag. It was one of the last things he said. He said, 'Make sure Brett gets the van and the tech bag. And the client list.' The pool cleaning business is yours, Brett. If you want it."

I smiled a little but it really kind of broke my heart. "I guess," I said, weakly. "I guess I'll need to do something for money after school and next summer. I guess it would be an honor, really."

"He also wanted you to have some money," she said. "Believe it or not, he had quite a bit stashed away. He didn't spend very much. Plus, this house is worth a little. Anyway, he mostly wanted me to use the money to help you pay for college, which I think will not be a problem. You're planning on going, right?"

"Uh, right," I said, not even really hearing her because I was so stunned by this information.

"And he also wanted you to have something up front. That's the way he said it. 'Give the kid something up front,' he said. 'Give him five grand. He'll like that. He loves money, poor guy.'" Linda smiled again. "He laughed when he said that, but then he kept insisting that it was true. He kept saying 'Poor kid, he loves money.'"

I wasn't quite sure if this was a compliment, but Linda quickly understood my confusion.

"You made quite an impression on him," she said. "He really loved you. Thought you were 'one strange kid.' And that's about as high a compliment as he's ever paid to anyone."

I kind of smiled. What a funny guy that Alfie was. And I kind of laughed, except that I also started crying because the whole thing just made me so incredibly sad again. It made me sad that Alfie thought of me as he was dying, that he thought I was a strange kid. It made me sad because I wished he were back so we could go clean pools together and goof off and drive around in his van.

"I don't know what to say," I finally said. "This is all so

strange. I don't know what to say. I don't know what to think about what Alfie left me."

"Well, you'll probably need to spend some of your cash on insuring the van, and maybe fixing it up. It looks a little broken down."

"And there's the tech bag," I said, appreciating the distraction of the pool business. "Got to buy more chlorine."

"You're a business owner now, Brett."

"I guess I am."

"My father really cared about you, Brett. He thought you were funny, and smart. And I know he loved working with you. He told me so."

"That's nice to know," I said. "That's nice to know."

And it was nice to know. Or maybe I should say that it was nice to hear. It was nice to hear because the truth is that I already knew it. I already knew what Alfie thought of me.

45 As I left Alfie's house that afternoon, I thought about how strange everything was. Linda gave me five hundred dollars in cash, and said she'd give me the rest after Alfie's affairs were finalized. I promised Linda that I'd help her with the sale, and then I said good-bye and stumbled out of the house, looking at the keys to the pool van, which was now mine, and thinking about how terrible and strange all this was.

It's funny how terrible things put everything in perspective. Like, someone you care about dies and you feel like nothing matters, like all the things that were driving you crazy just seem pointless. I couldn't help but think about how brokenhearted I had been about Nicole and what a joke all that seemed to be after Alfie died. My affection for her now seemed so senseless. Alfie was a friend. Nicole was a fantasy. Trivial fantasies like Nicole just didn't seem to matter anymore. Nothing seemed to matter, and I suddenly felt a strange sort of freedom, like a lot of the things that had been bugging me disappeared. I was still sad. But sad in a very concrete and meaningful way.

But by the time I got to the van in Alfie's driveway, I began to think about something else. It wasn't really that nothing mattered. Maybe all the dumb stuff floated away. But that left another feeling, a feeling that there were many things that mattered a great deal that I had to address immediately. I felt like I had really let some things slide that were actually really important to me. The main thing—the only thing, really, at that moment—was my father.

As I climbed into the pool van and put the key in the ignition

I decided I had to make a stop before I went home. I drove down Gleebe Avenue, on to Mason, and then on to the highway headed north. Had to go to Hartsville. I didn't really know why, or what I wanted to say, but I knew I wanted to see my father and when the thought occurred to me to go I just got on the highway and went.

I called my mom from the road to tell her where I was headed. I know she was worried about me. I hadn't had my license for that long and now I was driving around alone in the middle of nowhere. Under other circumstances she would have said something like, "Brett, you get home this minute."

But she knew I was upset and, more importantly, I think she was willing to accept my crazy behavior because it involved my father.

All she said was, "Call me as soon as you check into the hotel. You'll have to wait till tomorrow to see your dad. It'll be too late by the time you get there tonight."

It all seemed very strange to me. It was one of those moments I had been having in the past year where I suddenly became conscious of my surroundings and of who I was. It was like moving out of my house or seeing the judge send my father to prison. I became very, very aware. It was strange. I suddenly had a driver's license, a van, and enough cash to check into a hotel on my own. I was visiting my dad of my own free will. I was a business owner, of all things. Very strange.

By the time I got to Hartsville, I was exhausted. It's actually tiring to drive for five hours. You'd think it would be easy since all you do is sit there. But it was tiring. You stare at the same thing the whole time, you don't eat anything but junk, and your eyes hurt so bad they water. I always thought road trips looked like fun. Not this one.

When I got to the hotel, I called my mom again, just to tell her that I was alive. She likes to know that I'm alive. Then I went to bed. I listened to my mom tell me something or other, then I turned on the TV, got into bed, and fell asleep before I even closed my eyes.

46 So getting into a jail to see someone isn't as easy as you might think. I guess my mom was jabbering about how to do it when I called her from the hotel, but I clearly wasn't paying attention. You have to have permission to even ask permission to see someone at the Hartsville Prison. And then they've got to talk to the person you're visiting to see if he wants to see you.

"Of course he wants to see me, you fool," I said to the guy who was grilling me. "I'm his son." Actually, I didn't say "you fool." But I said the rest.

"We still have to ask him. And I need ID."

That was easy. "Here's one brand-new driver's license," I said.

The guy took the ID and then disappeared behind a door, and I didn't see him for another hour. And that's no exaggeration. Finally he came back and said that I could see my dad in the afternoon, after lunch.

"But he's my dad," I yelled. "I don't understand this. Why can't I just see him now?"

"Your dad's a criminal, son, and this is a prison. Things are a little different around here."

What a joke. But I guess he had a point.

I got fried chicken for lunch and ate like nine pieces. When I'm sad, no kind of food passes my lips. When I'm nervous, I eat like a horse.

Anyway, I stuffed my face and went back to the prison. My appointment time was two-thirty.

I drove into the parking lot at about five past two and was in the waiting room outside the visiting room by two-fifteen. And then I really started getting nervous. Like, nervous I-could-eat-a-whole-bucket-of-chicken nervous. Why? Well, for all the obvious reasons, not least of which was that I still had no idea why I was there. I had come to Hartsville because it struck me as the right thing to do, because I was feeling like I needed to pull things together. But who knew what that meant?

Not me. I mean, really, I had no idea what to say. I didn't feel like bursting into tears and telling my dad I loved him. In fact, I kind of felt like insulting him some more. It crossed my mind several times to tell him he was still an idiot and a loser. Even when the guard told me to enter the visiting room, I thought about telling my dad he was a loser. Wouldn't that be funny? Brett goes crazy and drives all the way to Hartsville just to tell his dad that he's a big fat idiot. But that's not what happened.

This is what happened: I didn't say anything mean and I didn't blubber about how much I loved him. I sat down and told my dad I was glad to see him and then I told him all about Alfie, how I found him, how he died, and how it was the saddest and weirdest thing that I had ever been through. I told him how it seemed like nothing made any sense to me anymore because the things I counted on in the world kept disappearing.

My dad listened to my story all the way through and told me that he wished he had gotten to know Alfie better, and then he told me a story about a friend of his who died in college, and how he still thinks of this guy every day, and how life seems to get more chaotic and mysterious the older he gets.

"For instance, getting tackled in your own kitchen by a bunch of cops is pretty strange," he said. "I may have deserved it. But I never expected it. I never expected things to just crumble around me like they did. Life is strange and it just keeps getting stranger." And then Dad told me more about prison and how weird it was there and how weird all the other prisoners were, and I told Dad more stories about Alfie and how I was now the proud owner of Moore Pool Cleaners and how I'd send him a jar of pickled green beans if the prison guards would allow it.

"They're the best," I told him. "You'd die if you tasted the pickled cauliflower. Disgusting. Fast Burger disgusting. But the beans are incredible. You've never tasted anything like them." And after telling more stories and after raving more about the pickled green beans and after talking about all sorts of other stuff, a guard finally came in to tell us that the hour was up.

I was a little afraid that things might get emotional about that time. I was afraid because it was the last thing I wanted. I decided that there would be nothing worse than a whole bunch of emotional pronouncements to blow the visit. But there weren't lots of emotional pronouncements. The emotion took on its own kind of simple expression. Because there were definitely emotions. I can tell you that. But the only thing we said was good-bye. My dad stood up and said, "Good-bye, Brett."

And I said, "Good-bye, Dad."

And then he said, "This was really great. It was really great to see you."

And I said the same. "It was really great," I said. "I'll see you again soon." And then that was it. Better that way than lots of senseless bawling that didn't mean anything. I know that men get yelled at in this day and age for not being able to express their emotions. But you can't tell me our emotions weren't expressed. You just can't. Trust me. Me telling my dad it was great to see him meant way more than a hundred billion "I love you's" ever would. That's just the way we were.

47 So, just think of all the lessons I've learned. You might imagine that I've grown as a human being, that all the struggle has made me a better person. Well, that's probably right. But who knows what I would have been like if my dad never got busted. Maybe I'd have learned the same lessons.

Yes, it's common wisdom that pain and hardship build character. But I'd like to propose some new common wisdom. Life is great when you have lots of money. I know. Money isn't everything. But I would have been much happier if I could have learned about life while napping in front of a wide-screen TV or listening to my five-thousand-dollar stereo. And think about the lessons I could have learned if I had gotten the new car my dad always promised me. That would have taught me a lesson or two—driving an expensive car that was my very own. Think of what I would have learned.

And so, along those lines, let me make a final snotty comment: as far as I'm concerned, I still hate Dad for blowing everything and losing the house and the pool. That's a fact.

But maybe I hate him in a different way than I thought. I hate the crap he pulled. But I don't hate everything about him. It's hard to say that I like anything about him. That is, it would be hard to make a list. But I guess there's a kind of love that doesn't really come with a list.

Like, say you've got a bratty son who's never learned a thing, is always rude, is definitely lazy, and won't ever admit he's wrong. Ever. Do you stop loving him? Nope. You make sandwiches for him and lend him the car and take him to swimming lessons and even buy him stuff. Why is that? It's a very puzzling phenomenon. But the phenomenon is a fact. A guy can do something stupid and ruin your life, but you still love him for no reason. No reason at all.

But if there is a reason, it might be because the guy who messed up your life also happens to love you and to need you, and if you stab him in the back, he's finished. You don't have many people like that in the world—people who need you and whom you need—and the ones you do have can disappear with no warning at all. So if you want a reason why any part of me still loves my father, it's that. Call it loyalty. In fact, I'm making loyalty part of the pool cleaner's oath, which I'm currently formulating because I'm hiring an assistant and he's going to have to do everything I say or he's gone, gone like I was outta Fast Burger, gone. Alfie's got a legacy in Glenwood and I'm going to make sure it doesn't get trampled on. Any guy who's going to work for me is going to have to know that right off the bat, or he's gone. Anyway.

When I got back from prison after visiting Dad, I pulled the van up in front of the house. My sister and Aunt Mary were sitting in the living room when I walked in, and they both jumped up to hug me.

"Enough, already," I said, although it felt good to hug them.

In about five minutes, my mother came in from work and the whole hugging thing started up again.

"OK. OK. Enough," I said, but, again, it felt good.

And then my mom asked me if I'd come in the kitchen and tell her about Dad while she made dinner. I told her the story of my trip and complained that the drive to Hartsville was a big fat hassle and that my little trip up north didn't mean I was going to visit Dad any more than was absolutely necessary. But my mom just smiled and said that I could make my own decisions. I just nodded, as though she hardly needed to tell me that, and then I decided that maybe I could tone down my obnoxious attitude a bit. But slowly, and on my own terms. No need to overdo it, I thought. No need to get all sentimental. Nope. No need for that.